7/19

D0045660

The
Problim
Children

CARNIVAL
CATASTROPHE

Also by Natalie Lloyd:
The Problim Children

The Problim Children

CARNIVAL CATASTROPHE

NATALIE LLOYD

INTERIOR ILLUSTRATIONS BY
JÚLIA SARDÀ

KATHERINE TEGEN BOOKS
An Imprint of HarperCollins Publishers

NORTHERN PLAINS
PUBLIC LIBRARY
Ault, Colorado

Katherine Tegen Books is an imprint of HarperCollins Publishers.

The Problim Children: Carnival Catastrophe
Text copyright © 2019 by HarperCollins Publishers
Illustrations copyright © 2019 by Júlia Sardà
All rights reserved. Printed in the United States of America.
No part of this book may be used or reproduced in any manner whatsoever
without written permission except in the case of brief quotations embodied in
critical articles and reviews. For information address HarperCollins Children's
Books, a division of HarperCollins Publishers, 195 Broadway, New York, NY
10007.
www.harpercollinschildrens.com

Library of Congress Control Number: 2019935136
ISBN 978-0-06-242824-0

Typography by Carla Weise
19 20 21 22 23   PC/LSCH   10 9 8 7 6 5 4 3 2 1
❖
First Edition

TO HANNAH PEMBERTON,

because she is smart, creative, loving,
and kind—a true beauty.

Mona Problim

Monday's child is fair of face,

Tuesday's child is full of grace,

Toot Problim

Wendell Problim

Wednesday's child is full of woe,

Thursday's child has far to go,

Thea Problim

Friday's child is
loving and giving,

Frida Problim

Sal Problim

Saturday's child works
hard for a living,

Sundae Problim

But the child who's born
on the Sabbath day is
good and wise in every way.

—Anonymous

The
Problim
Children

CARNIVAL
CATASTROPHE

Prologue

The wind came as a night visitor, sneaking through the town of Lost Cove like a clumsy bandit. Knocking boats against each other in the harbor, pushing over trash cans, tossing tree limbs into the street, and swirling across the barren land where a river used to be. A purple-tailed squirrel sleeping in a tall magnolia tree on Main Street startled awake. It was not afraid of this weather . . . but it was definitely curious.

Squirrels know that the sea wind carries all sorts of invisible things. That's why it's so restless. The wind carries wishes that never made it to the stars. Questions called out that will never be answered. Ghost stories. Ghosts, even. Sometimes. This particular wind had no ghosts tangled up inside it. But it did carry a warning. The squirrel felt it.

At House Number Seven, the wind burst through an upstairs window with a huff and a puff and a roar. It billowed down the stairs, all the way to the basement, and whispered over the face of a dark-haired girl as she dreamed.

Dreamed of her mama—a rugged adventurer wearing coveralls and a bulging backpack. She was standing in front of the mouth of a deep cave. A strange, warm breeze rustled up from the cavernous depths as the woman steadied herself. She stepped into that darkness.

The girl woke with a start. Her ears adjusted to the howling wind.

She tiptoed upstairs to see if there was an open window. Her siblings would be scared if they saw her, and she didn't care to wake them tonight. (Though she did love to play tricks on them in the dark.) She had a ghostly look about her, they said. Skin as pale as moonlight on snow. Hair the color of midnight. She felt like a ghost sometimes too, especially because she loved spooky nights like this so much. She walked to the window and let the wind ruffle her hair.

The wind is the wolf, she thought.

And then: I'm like a wolf too.

The girl shoved the window closed and turned the latch just as two circus spiders smacked against the glass. They rubbed their heads with their tentacles and set to work swinging from corner to corner. Circus spiders excel at many tricks, but catching rumors in their web is their most notorious trait.

And that particular storm had many rumors tossed around inside it.

Rumor bubbles, trembling in the breeze, began playing tiny moving pictures of the strangest ideas:

A dark ship on the sea, bobbing closer to shore.

A man in a long trench coat, standing on the bow of the ship, watching. Waiting. Looking for a way in. Or looking for someone.

Seven someones?

Revenge doesn't age, you see. It's as old as the wind. And it grows in power, like a storm over the sea.

If the Problim children had listened that night, just a bit more closely, they might have been prepared for everything about to happen. But they did not hear the warning. They only heard the wind. By morning, the rumors had faded away. The spiders, having done all they could, wove webby white sleeping bags in the trees and fell asleep.

Of course, the children noticed the wild weather in town. Everyone did.

"It started last night," said the dark-haired girl.

"The wind brought the storm. It gave me strange dreams."

The squirrel heard this. It flicked its tail, and shivered.

Because some dreams—even terrible ones—are bound to be true.

Knock and Look

Monday's rain fell silver and sideways so that no person—or squirrel—roaming around Lost Cove stayed dry. They all tried, though. People dashed from shops to parked cars with soggy newspapers covering their heads. Or with hoods pulled so low over their faces they could barely see. Noah Wong's mom made him carry an umbrella to skateboard in the park, but the wind flicked it inside out as soon as he opened it. A tug-of-war with the wind ensued. (Noah lost.)

The sky had gurgled storm warnings all morning long, but that didn't matter. Excitement sizzled along the puddled streets. Smiles stretched across dripping faces. Everyone in town seemed to be out and about, and thrilled.

Especially two girls presently riding their bicycles down the sidewalks.

"Another puddle! GLORY!" Sundae Problim veered for a deep muddy mess ahead of her, sliced through the middle, and squealed as muck slopped up all over her jeans and shoes. She howled with happy laughter. Her younger sister, Mona Problim, kicked along nearby on a scooter.

Mona rolled her eyes at Sundae's latest exclamation: GLORY. That was her new thing; Sundae shouted the word all the time these days. Mona quietly enjoyed the satisfying swish of her tires through the puddle, and the way mud felt when it speckled her arms. So refreshing.

"Rain *is* my favorite weather," Mona called out. "Nothing like a nice long walk in a thunderstorm."

A passel of elderly ladies in matching yellow parkas watched the girls from the crosswalk. Sundae and Mona stopped in front of them, waiting for the light to change. Mona couldn't help overhearing their conversation. (Actually, she could help it. But Mona liked to be acutely aware of her surroundings at all times. She never knew when such intel would come in handy for the pranks she was constantly plotting against her siblings.)

"That Problim girl there—the scary one—she's so pretty, isn't she?" one of them whispered behind her.

Mona considered this. Scary was fine. Scary was interesting, at least. Pretty was the absolute least interesting thing about anyone. Mona sighed and concentrated on the "Walk" sign, willing the light to flip. Why was pretty always one of the first things people said about girls? Pretty—as if that was the ultimate most excellent achievement in the entire world.

"It's nonsense," Mona mumbled to Fiona, the Venus flytrap nestled in the front basket of her scooter.

"What?" Sundae asked.

"Nothing. Just talking to Fiona."

"How enchanting!" Sundae said. "Every living thing loves to be spoken to and acknowledged—"

Thankfully, the sign flickered—"WALK"—before Sundae could go any further. The girls zoomed their bike (plus scooter) to a stop in front of the Better Donuts shop. The neon-pink "Open" sign flickered extra bright against the darkening sky. Sundae skipped toward the entry. (Mona did not skip any-where, ever.) Dorothy, the owner, met them at the door with her hands on her hips.

"STOP," Dorothy commanded. "Wipe your paws before you come in my shop." She pointed to the mat, then to a sign affixed to the building beside the door. "See here? 'No mud. No mess. No cell phones.'"

Sundae blinked. "I understand not wanting cell phones. But . . . mud is nature's love letter to all of us. Why not bring some of the joy of nature indoors?"

As Sundae began telling Dorothy about all the creatures whose natural habitats were mud, Mona shimmied past her sister and into the bakery. The room smelled like warm cinnamon. Families and couples sat clustered around tables. Coffee sputtered from a machine in the corner. In the back of the room, fresh donuts zoomed off one conveyor belt, plopping down onto another. Then each one passed underneath a waterfall of white icing.

Rrrrr. Now it was Mona's stomach rumbling, just as loud as the morning storm-sky. She and Sundae had been up early—Glory!—to go knock on doors. While this activity could have been fun in its own right, there was a reason for all the knocking.

A very important reason.

But for now, they needed a donut break.

Mona slid into a corner table beside her siblings, hoping one of them had a pastry she could swipe. Alas, they did not. Rain bubbled on her older brother Sal's gardening tools. He hadn't been there long. None of them had.

"Well?" Sal asked.

Mona shrugged. "We didn't find anything. Let's have breakfast."

"Forget breakfast!" Sal said. "We have a family meeting scheduled."

She sighed. Mona wished she'd brought some circus spiders with her, to sneak a donut off the line. That would have been a wonderful challenge. Wendell Problim was presently standing guard over the donuts. He wore his new green apron and hairnet. He watched each circle of deliciousness roll past, counting them all, making sure they were iced proportionally.

Wendell had been an intern at Better Donuts for a week now, and Sal had already helped him design a quicker conveyor belt. Wendell's first job was counting inventory, but he hoped to work his way up to apprentice decorator. Mona couldn't wait until Wendell had access to the fryer, because that meant she'd have access too. She'd already thought about how many things she would like to deep-fry just to see how they'd turn out:

A boot.

A book.

One of Sal's plants.

Maybe a spider.

Something bit Mona's thumb. Hard. A tiny, blue-legged circus spider glared up at her.

"I was kidding," she whispered. And then she grinned. "In fact, I'm so glad you're here. See that donut over there . . . ?"

"Are you even paying attention, Mona?" Sal asked.

"Yes! I already told you that we didn't find anything."

Sal rested his drippy head in his hands. "Neither did I. I knocked on almost every door along the Battery and . . . nothing."

"Same," admitted Thea, Wendell's twin. "I'm starting to worry." (Not a surprise, Mona thought. Thea was always only ever worried. Mona considered trying to comfort her sister, maybe reaching out and patting her shoulder. But sometimes Mona scared her siblings if she moved too quickly.) Baby Toot snuggled in Thea's arms, napping. Frida Problim was also at the table but she wasn't really sitting. She was upside-downing in the chair. Only her sneakers were visible. Her muffled voice came from under the table:

"We've knocked
and spied
and searched in nooks.
There's nowhere else that's left to look!"

"Agree," Mona said. "We must be reading the clue wrong."

For a week now, the Problim children had been trying to find seven twigs. Bony, plain-looking white twigs that looked like any other branch—except for the flecks of gold at the edges. Those twigs would all snap together into something called a water witch, which would lead them to a treasure beyond measure. They only had three out of the seven twigs left to find.

"Maybe *you* misread the clue," Sal suggested. "But knock and look sounds very straightforward to me. Like it's hidden on a door somewhere. So I say we carry on as planned. We haven't searched the East Side of Lost Cove yet."

Thea cuddled Toot close. "Sal's right. We have to keep trying." She lowered her voice. "I've seen sevens everywhere. I really feel like something terrible is about to happen." She sighed. "We must carry on. As Midge Lodestar says: Every day is a . . ."

"Good day for a taco," they all said in unison.

Mona smirked, just a little (which was usually as close as she got to a smile). None of Thea's life mottoes made such sense, but Thea said them so triumphantly. So sincerely. Mona appreciated that about Thea, the way she made her way through fear and worry by finding something good to focus on. Mona, on the other hand, enjoyed the process of fear itself. Fear made her feel more alive, more brave, even.

Fear. Like the way Mama Problim had looked in Mona's dreams last night. The way she steeled her shoulders and marched ahead, into that darkness, looking for something. . . .

Mona's belly gargled. Loudly. Forget the clue

(for now). Forget her weird dreams. Breakfast was top priority. She sat taller in her chair to check the progress of the great donut heist. At last! One donut did appear to be magically crawling off the conveyor belt.

"Mo." Sal said her name like a warning. "Why do you keep looking over there?"

"No reason." Mona whipped her head back around to the sound of the door as it jingled open. Several smiling—wet—customers scrambled inside. Mona noticed hordes of people bustled past the shop's big window. So many people out and about on a stormy day.

"Why *is* it so crowded in Lost Cove?" she asked. She appreciated rotten weather as much as anyone, but still. "It's a Monday. Why aren't people working?"

WHAP!

"The Lost Cove Corn Dog Carnival starts tomorrow!" Dorothy said, slamming a copy of the local newspaper down on the table. "It's been called a festival up until this year. But the busybodies who plan the thing say *carnival* sounds more exciting." She rolled her eyes. "Everybody's off work! It's a whole week of fun. Have you seen this?"

THE 77TH ANNUAL
LOST COVE CORN DOG CARNIVAL!

Who will brave the
PIRATES' CAVERNS?

Who will bake this year's
PRIZED PIE?

Who will make the year's
BEST ART?

Who will be crowned this year's
CORN DOG PRINCESS?

"That sounds terrible," Mona said bluntly. "None of these contests look remotely dangerous. Why would anyone be interested?"

"A p-pie competition!" Wendell said, startling them all.

"An art contest!" Sal pulled the paper toward him.

Mona snatched the paper. "Too bad we have a

mystery to solve right now. Maybe next year."

The Problim children nodded in sad agreement.

Dorothy nodded too. "It's a shame you can't participate. It's the biggest event in town, happens every year. And it's not just special on account of the carnival. It's special because of the Pirates' Caverns—islands of caves just off the beach where the carnival is held. Nobody's allowed over in the caverns, usually. They can be real dangerous when the tide washes in. But! During carnival week, the water gets low enough to step inside those caves and see where pirates used to hide out from the sea police. Plus, it's real pretty. When it's not flooded."

Dorothy looked around, then leaned low and whispered, "Last year, Desdemona O'Pinion got a city citation for trying to snorkel into one of them."

The Problim children glanced at one another. They knew *all* about Desdemona O'Pinion and her (mostly) rotten family. She had tried (and nearly succeeded) at getting rid of the Problim children so she could find their grandpa's treasure herself.

What could she have wanted in that cave? Mona wondered.

And then another thought settled in her brain, a very uncomfortable one. She remembered last night's dream again. Mama Problim, wandering into a cave alone, searching for something. So many caves lately. So many storms. Mona smirked. Danger was afoot. And she liked danger.

"Arf!"

Biscuit, the small, furry dog belonging to their new friend Violet O'Pinion, flounced into the room, tracking mud everywhere (much to Dorothy's dismay). Violet was an O'Pinion too, but most of the Problim children seemed to trust her anyway. (Most, but not Mona.) Biscuit pounced up onto an empty chair, and Sal reached for the scroll attached to the collar around her neck.

Come quickly!
I have a brainstorm!
Bring me a donut.
—Violet

"Problims, pile up!" Thea shouted. And then she realized her lap was empty. "Um . . . where's Toot?"

16

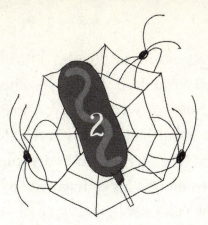

A Catastrophe of Donuts

Mona wrinkled her nose as an eggy-smelling #4[1] fart, courtesy of Toot Problm, permeated the atmosphere of the donut shop.

"He's getting iced," Sal said.

"Oh, adorable!" Sundae pulled a camera from her backpack and ran to take pictures for the family scrapbook. "Go stand beside him, Wendell!"

"Go get him off my machinery!" Dorothy bellowed. Everyone in the shop turned to see what was happening. (A collective "aww" echoed when they

---

1 #4: The Stink of Dread: A fart born of anxiety, foretelling a terrible event. Smells faintly of rotten eggs and vomit.

saw Toot playing in the donuts.)

Wendell scrambled for his brother. But Toot speedy-crawled over the conveyor, knees squishing into every donut blocking his path. Mona smirked with pride. Toot was the most adventurous Problim by far. She admired his courage, not to mention his ability to wreak utter havoc.

"Don't pull him away yet!" Mona called to Wendell. "Let him complete the mission!"

"He's trying to rescue one of the circus spiders," Sal said. And then he glared at Mona. "Why is a circus spider trying to carry a donut off the machine?"

"Perhaps it was hungry," Mona said innocently. It wasn't a lie. Not exactly.

"Ears up, Buttercups!" Frida shouted, pouncing onto the tabletop.

"It's Tootykins the Brave!
There is no creepy-crawly creature
that Tooty will not save!"

She pulled her fox-eared hoodie up over her head. And stood still as a statue.

Wendell had nearly reached Toot when he slid

in a puddle of glaze and slammed into the floor. As Toot finally reached for the tiny spider (who was still hiding under a donut), his hand came down on a blob of strawberry icing. He tasted it and went very still, eyes glazing over in pure love and adoration. The spider forgotten, Toot stood, tottering toward the icing waterfall with one hand outstretched like a desperate sugar zombie. With the other hand, he held on to the top of the machine for balance. Only a blinking red button made him stop. And squeal. And pop a #200.[2]

"Looks like he's going to test the turbo button," Sal said. "Just leave him alone, Wendell. Don't you want to see how it works?"

"M-maybe not right this s-second," Wendell said, trying to regain his balance on the slippery floor.

"NOPE!" Dorothy hollered.

But Toot clapped his hand down on the blinky. And donuts began firing off the line at a rate of seven per second. Donuts launched into the room and bounced off the walls. One whopped Sal in the

---

2 **#200**: The Toot of Intrigue: A faint, lingering aroma that helps Toot concentrate on unusual, yet enticing, bits of information. Smells like old books, soft cheese, and mildew.

forehead. One landed on the brim of Mr. Seifert's cowboy hat. Another donut shot out the front door, into the open mouth of Noah Wong as he was about to say hello.

Donuts pelted into the street like speedy-delicious Frisbees.

"It's raining donuts!" someone yelled from outside.

"Glory!" Sundae shouted as she ran out to take pictures. Then she began dancing in the downpour of sprinkles.

"Get Sir Farts-a-Lot OFF my machinery!" Dorothy hollered.

Donuts stuck to the ceiling and the doors before Wendell finally reached the crank, turned off the machine, and lifted his baby brother (spider safely perched on his shoulder) away from the conveyor belt. Miss Dorothy, presently covered in donuts and squishy icing, simply stared at them. And blinked. For a moment, there was silence.

And then, Toot sputter-blasted a #14[3] and gave himself a round of applause. Mona applauded too. And so did everyone in the room.

---

3 #14: The Bon Appétit: Mellow smell of the kitchen after cooking stinky fish. Released when Toot is ready to enjoy a delicious meal.

"Here." Sundae handed her sticky camera to Dorothy. "Will you take a picture of us all together for our family scrapbook, please? This is Wendell's first day at work!"

The Problim children, all covered in icing, confectioner's sugar, and sprinkles, huddled together. With arms looped around each other, they smiled. (Mona smirked.) Dorothy sighed, and snapped the shot.

"Wait!" Frida shouted. She ran in front of her siblings and held an imaginary camera over her chest.

"One more time,
go back!
Restart!
I want a picture for my heart."

Up the street, a large, dark SUV was parked with the lights on, windshield wipers sloshing. Behind the wheel sat a woman in dark sunglasses, despite the absence of any sun. She drummed her long fingernails against the steering wheel and smiled— just barely—as the Problim kids scampered outside. They looked so dirty, so *disgusting*, covered in mud as they climbed on their bikes and scooters and rode away. Toward home, maybe. Toward another clue, most likely.

"Be patient, Desdemona," the woman reminded herself. A cold wind blew down the street, sending clusters of leaves scraping across the windshield. Desdemona sighed, and grinned. Yes, her last plan had failed. But she was a resourceful woman. Not to mention an observant one. All she had to do now was wait and the Problim children would lead her to the treasure.

A boom of thunder made her shiver and pull her cardigan tighter around her chest. The wilder those wretched children behaved, the wilder these strange storms blew around town. Did they know yet exactly what they were capable of?

Desdemona took a steadying breath. As soon as they found the treasure, she would snatch it. And then she would find a way to get them out of her town for good. Patience, she reminded herself.

High in the magnolia tree above the car sat an equally observant purple-tailed squirrel. It shivered on the edge of the limb, remembering its vow to protect the Problim family no matter what. The squirrel knew to watch out for Desdemona O'Pinion, of course. But the squirrel also looked toward the sea, that dangerous place where the coast met the sky. Desdemona was a villain, no doubt about it. But the world was so big past that horizon. And there were worse villains out there somewhere, always searching for the seven.

Return of the Girl with Wings

Violet O'Pinion leaned over the desk in her bedroom, studying the scribbles in a spiral notebook. The wings on her shoulders painted shadows on the wall in front of her. Her wing shadows were the prettiest art she'd ever had in her room, she decided. They weren't real wings, of course, only paper, but that didn't matter. They helped her think. Even better, they helped her imagine. Today she needed her mind and her imagination to work together and solve a clue for her new friends, the Problim family. But one of the many plants blooming in Violet's room kept stealing her attention:

The droopy twig-tree-thing growing in a pot on the desk.

That plant—she thought it was a tree, *maybe*—sat snug in a bundle of soil. The best soil. She'd watered it. Sung to it. Whispered stories right beside it, just for the plant to hear. The plant was blooming, technically. The weird thing is that it bloomed downward. This was fine, of course. Some plants, and people, bloom differently than others.

But no matter where she moved her tiny twig-tree, it pointed toward the floor. Sometimes it rose a little. Then, later on, she would actually hear it bending— a soft, steady *creeeeeak* like a porch door swinging shut. Sometimes she saw the plant's shadow moving silently over the wall, as if the end of that plant was connected to some kind of invisible magnet below the floor.

Biscuit had dug up the plant almost a week ago, possibly from Sal Problim's garden. Since then, Violet pored over books and articles trying to figure out what, exactly, Biscuit had discovered.

"It's time to ask the Problims about it," Violet mumbled as she made notes in her scientific notebook. She had hoped to solve the plant mystery without the help of her new friends. Solving problems was the fun part. That's something her new friends had taught her.

Fwump!

Wendell Problim landed outside Violet's tower window, holding Biscuit securely in his arms. Wendell's sister, Mona, zoomed across the zip line next and landed elegantly beside her brother. Mona seemed to be in a good mood; she even had a hint of a smile on her face. Probably the rain, Violet decided. Mona Problim reminded Violet of a tiny thundercloud: pretty but kind of scary.

Violet reached for her purified air helmet, which she had to wear before letting her new friends in the room. Well. Her new *friend*. Violet had connected with Wendell Problim immediately. Mona had threatened to feed Violet to her Venus flytrap the first time they'd met. Based on the smirk on Mona's face, she still didn't like Violet very much. It wasn't like they had any reason to distrust Violet.

And yet . . .

Quickly, in a movement so swift they wouldn't see, Violet reached for a framed picture on her desk and hid it in her drawer.

"Be nice to V-Violet," Wendell said to Mona. The two of them watched from outside as Violet shuffled around and clicked her helmet in place.

"Why?" Mona didn't say it rudely. She was truly curious. It was that word—*nice*—that irked her so much. Why did people always tell her to be nice? Just because she was blunt, did that mean she wasn't nice? And besides, it wasn't like she had any reason to be rude or mean to Violet. Violet was an O'Pinion, but she seemed to be a harmless one. There was no fun in tormenting her. No, Mona had something far more important to do inside the O'Pinion house tonight.

"Just a second," Violet called out to them.

Mona and Wendell stood up on the ledge, preparing to jump inside, when a sudden force zoomed into them. "Ugh," they said in unison, as their faces were smooshed against the glass.

"Excuse me," Thea said sweetly from behind them. "So sorry! The zip line is slick and speedy when wet."

"Way to make an entrance," Mona grumbled.

"Thank you," Thea said sweetly. "Midge Lodestar says if you're going to make an entrance, you might as well ask for the double combo."

Mona knocked on the window. "Please hurry, Violet. My sister is trying to life-coach me."

"Hello! Good morning," Violet cooed as she pulled open the window and reached for her dog. Biscuit pounced into Violet's arms and licked her bubble mask happily.

Wendell pulled a squashed bag from inside his coat. "S-strawberry donut for you! S-squished but still delicious!"

"Thank you, Wendell! How's your internship going?"

"Big adv-venture this morning," Wendell said as he jumped into the room. "It's all g-good at Better Donuts."

Thea jumped in next. "And the Lost Cove Corn Dog Carnival begins tomorrow! Everybody in town is thrilled!"

"I don't understand why," Mona said, sitting down on the window ledge. She folded her hands in her lap. "People can make their own carnival in their own yard whenever they want." Her siblings had had a festival, carnival, and circus all in the same day, in their backyard. That was a pretty average Wednesday for the Problim family.

"Not everybody gets to be a Problem," Violet said with a wistful sigh. She cuddled Biscuit close. "I wish I could go to the carnival. Every year, I hear the music. I read stories in the paper about the parade—"

Mona raised an eyebrow. "There's a parade?" Mona'd always dreamed of making her own float! Full of black flowers, spiders, perhaps a snake or two curled around a well-dressed skeleton.

"Yes," Violet told her. "And all sorts of contests."

Mona shrugged. "All of those look dull. There's not even a knife-throwing competition."

"And there are so many people who come from miles away," Violet continued. "Sometimes people bring lovely old ships and dock them in the harbor. Imagine how pretty that looks in the fog! Plus, I like people-watching."

People. This time an honest-to-goodness grin stretched across Mona's face. She didn't like to people-watch. She liked to people-meddle. Wendell and Thea were always looking to make a new friend in the people they met. Mona was more interested in sizing people up to see if they were worthy opponents. "You've changed my perspective on the carnival, Violet O'Pinion."

"Opportunities for prankability will be endless."

Violet's helmet made her voice sound like a happy robot.

"It would have been a great fit for my strengths," Mona agreed, impressed by Violet's skills of deduction. A tremor of thunder sent a lovely shiver across her shoulders. "Oh, I do love a good storm."

"You remind me of a storm," Violet said. Whenever she spoke, tiny plumes of breath smoked against the inside of her helmet.

Mona rested her hand over her heart, surprised by the strange warmth blooming there. "I'm touched. It is one of my life goals to get struck by lightning."

"Oh." Violet's eyes widened. "Well . . . dream big, I guess." She pulled her scientific notebook off her desk.

"I'll make this quick. I just wanted to ask you about—"

"Shh—" Mona said to everyone.

The thunder had been muffled when Violet shut the window. But another sound filled the air around them: music, the soft scream of a violin. A few long strains of sound soared through the air before gently fading.

"That sounded like something ghosts would dance to," Mona said, raising an eyebrow. "Is that

Carly-Rue practicing for another pageant?"

"That's . . . not her," Violet said, with a nervous edge in her voice. "But she is downstairs, I think."

"Excellent," Mona cooed. This was exactly what she'd hoped to hear.

Carly-Rue O'Pinion, Mona's most formidable foe in all of Lost Cove, was somewhere on the floor beneath her. She still owed Carly-Rue a payback prank for nearly getting the family kicked out of town a week ago. This was Mona's chance, she realized, to observe her sparkly-skirt-wearing nemesis in the wild. To find her weakness. To plot a suitable revenge prank that the corn dog royal would never forget.

"M-Mona," Wendell said nervously. "Why are you s-smiling like th-that?"

"No reason," Mona declared. "Please hold off on sharing your discovery, Violet. I need a bathroom break."

The Enemy Wears Sparkles
(and a Discovery Is Made)

Mona eased down the tower-room stairs to the top floor of the O'Pinion mansion. Thick carpet muffled her steps. Three doors at the end of the hallway sent wedges of lemon-colored light into the darkness. The walls were covered in framed black-and-white family portraits. Tiny lights shone down on each print, as if they were priceless paintings in a museum gallery. One showed Carly-Rue in a pageant dress, holding a trophy, wearing a crown almost as tall as she was. Another photo showed Will O'Pinion, Carly-Rue's brother, sitting on a boat dock with his arm around a golden retriever.

Mona felt an icy zing in her heart as she looked

up at the next photo . . . because for a split second, she thought she was seeing herself. She bounced up on her tippy-toes and pressed her nose nearly to the glass to get a better look. Two little girls standing beside their bicycles—one girl's hair was dark. One was light. Written with a marker in the corner:

M + D = forever friends

"That's cheesy," Mona mumbled. And then a wretched, shrieking sound pulled her attention away from the picture. This wasn't the violin from earlier. This was a voice. A squeaky, high-pitched voice. Kind of like a cartoon mouse.

Mona eased farther down the hall, toward the first open door. She edged closer until she could just see inside.

Carly-Rue O'Pinion stood in front of the mirror in her room, wearing her most recent crown, twisting a shiny coil of hair around her finger. "I am so grateful for the opportunity to be your new corn dog princess AGAIN. This year, my platform is hand sanitizers on all school buses at all times. It's just common decency."

What was so bad about mud and germs, Mona thought. Both were delightful! Not only was Carly-Rue O'Pinion obviously narrow-minded, but she was also conniving.

A week ago, Carly-Rue had snuck onto the Problim property with her mom to lure Mona away from Toot. Desdemona snatched Toot and left him alone in the attic, near the Porch of Certain Death. Desdemona's plan had been for the Society for the Protection of Unwanted Children to see the Problim children scrambling out onto a wobbly, dangerous porch trying to save a baby. At the sight of it, they would send the seven away to seven different continents. The O'Pinions hadn't just tried to get rid of them. They'd tried to separate them.

Mona had decided then and there she would have to deal with them both: Desdemona and Carly-Rue. Teach them a lesson: when someone comes against any Problim, they come against her. Carly-Rue O'Pinion might be the reigning corn dog princess. But she—Mona Devona Elizabeth Problim the First—was the Queen of Prankdom.

It was almost time to retaliate. Almost time to get Carly-Rue back.

Patience, Mona reminded herself.

I'll see you soon, Carly-Rue, she thought. And she slipped back up the stairs.

Mona knocked on Violet's door to make sure her mask was in place.

"Come on in!" the winged girl cooed. When Mona pushed her way inside, she found the three of them, plus Biscuit, standing very still, facing Violet's desk.

"I was hoping to get your thoughts on my discovery," Violet was saying.

"And it's q-quite a d-discovery!" Wendell said. "C-come see, Mo."

Mona pushed through the trio and saw what held their attention: a plant.

A familiar-looking plant . . .

Mona raised an eyebrow, just slightly. "Ohhhh." And then her eyes narrowed. Now she was impressed! "Violet. You stole a bone-stick!"

"A what?" Violet looked up. "You mean my little tree? I didn't steal it. Biscuit carried it inside a few weeks ago. I've been trying to determine what it is."

"It's ours," Mona informed her.

"Sh-should we go get S-Sal?" Wendell asked nervously.

Mona's ears felt suddenly hot at the tips. Why did it matter if Sal was here? Why did everyone assume Sal was some expert when it came to magical twigs? "Sal is not the boss of this family," Mona said. "I am."

"No one is the boss," Thea said to her. "Our family is a democracy. But we should borrow this— if that's okay with you, Violet?—so we can go show everyone else."

"Please take it if it's yours," Violet said. "I would have given it to you already if I'd known."

"You've seen the bone-sticks, Violet," Mona said, cocking her head at the little winged O'Pinion. "You know what they look like. . . ."

"I didn't realize *this* was one of them!" Violet looked a little bit offended, but there was also a sudden flicker in her eyes. Mona saw it. Had Violet known, deep down, she was keeping something secret that belonged to the Problems? Violet straightened her wings. "What . . . what do the bone-sticks do exactly? I feel like I have a right to know."

"I'm not sure we can trust you," Mona said, not

rudely, but Thea still punched her in the arm.

"Desdemona already knows what they do," Thea said. "Haven't you seen her watching us?"

Then Thea looked directly at Violet. "Long story short: the twigs will all eventually snap together to create something called a water witch. And the water witch will lead us to a treasure Grandpa and his siblings found when they were kids: magical water. *Really* magical water."

Violet's eyes were wide and blinky. "Oh."

Mona crept closer to the plant to inspect it. Bone white, gold-tipped at the top. *Yes*, it had to be a bone-stick like the others. Why *was* it bending down . . . Mona wondered. None of the other bone-sticks had any give whatsoever.

"You say the little mop dog stole it from our yard?" Mona asked. "You don't know where in the yard she found it?"

Violet's cheeks flamed red. "Accusing sweet Biscuit of stealing is a low blow, Mona Problim! My dog isn't a thief! She was probably playing fetch with one of Sal's plants. I didn't think he would care if I planted it in here. Just take it back if it's yours!"

"Good idea," Mona said, snatching the plant off Violet's desk. She patted Biscuit's head as she walked past, commending the mop dog on this stealth thievery. Biscuit growled.

Violet crossed her arms as if she was waiting for something. "You won't get very far with that," she said.

Mona smirked. "Have you set a trap, Violet?" Now she was *really* impressed.

As Mona turned toward the window, she stumbled. But not because of any trap. The plant didn't just bloom down, like Violet said. It pulled Mona so hard toward the bedroom floor that her arms trembled trying to hold it. She began an invisible tug-of-war, yanking the plant to the window.

"Did you bewitch it?" Mona asked excitedly.

"What? No!"

"Wendell! Thea! Help me with Grandpa's *booone.*"

Violet's face scrunched. "Ew . . . please tell me that's not what it is."

"It's n-not a bone." Wendell rolled his eyes. "It's just a w-water w-witch."

Mona gritted her teeth and walked backward, pulling the plant across the floor. "The other ones don't do this. She did something to it."

"Excuse you." Violet came to her full (but still small) height and propped her hands on her hips.

Her wing shadows stretched across the walls as she stepped toward Mona. "I have only ever tried to help you."

Mona stood up straight, to look Violet in the eye. And then she forgot what she wanted to say to her because those wings were so close to her face. They had maps all over them. *Interesting.* "Why do you wear paper wings?" Mona asked. "You can't fly in them, can you?"

"M-Mona!" Wendell yelled at her. Which made no sense to Mona: she hadn't meant it mean! Not at all. She was truly curious. Violet seemed to understand this. Her shoulders relaxed a little. She smiled, kindly.

"These are magical wings," Violet said softly. "I made them out of worlds I'll visit someday. They make me brave from tip to tip, around the world and back again."

A fine explanation, Mona thought. Very noble. Perhaps Mona could make a small set of wings for Baby Toot and dress him like a little goblin. Teach him to hide all over the house and jump out and scare Sal when he least expected it. That would make for a lovely afternoon.

"Maybe we should talk to the plant," Thea said. "Like Sal talks to his plants. And convince it to come with us. Mona even talks to her flytrap sometimes." Mona glared at her sister.

Thea reached down and tickled the twig. "Hello, friend. May I pick you up? I'm going to take you home to all of your brothers and sisters. You'll all be together, exactly where you belong."

Mona blinked at her. "Sundae is a terrible influence on you, Thea."

But somehow, this seemed to work. Thea balanced the plant on her hip, as if it was Baby Toot. The tip of the twig still leaned toward the floor. But she was able to carry it, at least.

Wendell climbed into the window and took the plant from Thea. He looked like a sneaky thief perched in the frame.

"One th-thing about the tw-twigs," Wendell said to Violet. "Your g-grandfather is S-Stan O'P-P-Pinion, right?"

Violet stilled. Mona turned to watch her expression.

Violet's mouth quirked into a sad little grimace. "Yes."

"B-be c-careful ar-round him, ok-kay?"

"Why?" The question was a quick breath against Violet's mask.

"He's a villain," Mona said bluntly.

Thea gave her sister a gentle shove. "A good source, a reliable source, told us that he might be, you know. A *really* bad guy."

"Worse than Desdemona," Mona added. "If he finds this thing before we do, he'll do something bad with the treasure."

"So d-don't tell him or h-her about the tw-twigs, okay?"

Violet nodded but didn't actually promise with her words. Mona noticed this.

Mona also noticed the expression on Violet's face, like she was suddenly working a hard math problem in her head. Wendell didn't seem to care about any of that. He and Thea were so blindly trusting of everyone. Right now, they were staring at each other, twin-talking with big smiles on their faces.

"Great," Thea said as she bounced up into the window. "Oh!" She reached into her small backpack and pulled out a jar with holes poked into the top. Blue-legged spiders scurried around inside. "Here you go."

"Y-you s-said you wanted s-some circus spiders. F-for a project."

Violet took the jar with a smile as wide as if she'd been given a Christmas present. "Thank you."

"You're welcome," Thea called. She and Wendell zoomed across the street.

And then they were alone, Mona and the girl with wings.

Just as Mona was about to say good-bye, Violet spoke: "I wish you wouldn't write me off just because of my aunt. What she did to your family was awful. But I'm not her. I'm me. Sometimes you come off kind of cruel, Mona. But I don't think you are."

"Cruel?" Mona pretended Violet's words didn't sting, but they did. Cruel wasn't something she wanted to be. She was trying to be protective of her siblings . . . but maybe that came off the wrong way sometimes.

Mona considered her words carefully. "Your wings are cool, Violet."

She registered the quick look of shock on Violet's face, then climbed out the window and shut it behind her. Just before she zipped across the street, she looked back at Violet O'Pinion. The girl had pulled off her bubble mask. She held Biscuit safe in her arms. And she'd slunk down beside her door, listening to that sad violin music that was floating through the house again.

The plant had wanted something in that house; it leaned into it. Violet O'Pinion was doing the same thing, Mona realized.

When Sticks Collide

The storm outside the Problim house sounded like an upset tummy.

An upset tummy belonging to an angry giant. The sky gurgled, growled, and roared. Swirls of rain slashed at Mona, Wendell, and Thea Problim's face as they raced across the zip line and landed in the front yard.

"If I'd known the weather here was so dreamy, I'd have blown up the bungalow ages ago," Mona said. She searched the horizon for lightning like some people search for shooting stars. I'll make a wish on a lightning bolt, she thought. Why not? Stars sit still and twinkle. But lightning strikes and shimmers.

"I would rather be a lightning bolt than a shoot-ing star," she said to her siblings.

Wendell seemed confused. But Thea beamed. "Brilliant, Mona! Is that your life motto?"

Mona shrugged. Maybe it was.

"I like a d-dangerous storm as much as you do," Wendell assured her as he hoisted the plant on his hip. "But let's h-hurry so we can tell everybody what we f-found."

Mona groaned as she followed her brother through the front door of their house. Because tonight, the Problim house was not dark or bolt-y fun. It was warm and bright and smelled like the (slightly burnt) chocolate chip cookies someone had just pulled from the oven. Their sneakers squeaked across the marble floors as they ran into the library.

Toot and the family's pet pig, Ichabod, were mak-ing a book fort on the floor. Sundae was working at the corner desk with one of Mama Problim's old microscopes, sewing a small blanket for a wattabat she'd found in the backyard. The bat now rested in a sling around her chest. (Only Sundae could charm a wattabat, Mona thought. Usually those little fiends just bite and poop. They were formidable foes.) Frida sat curled in the window, playing her ukulele.

"FIRE!" Mona yelled. Her siblings looked up at her, excitement radiating in their eyes. Especially Sundae. She loved making her siblings practice fire evacuation.

"Just kidding." Mona shrugged. "Look." She pointed to the pot in Wendell's arms. "We found another *boooone*."

Wendell held the potted plant up like a trophy for his siblings to see. They cheered and ran for him to get a closer look. Frida squealed in happiness as she pounced from the window.

"Ears up, buttercups!
Wendell found a clue!
Go on Wendell,
rally the troops!
And tell us what to do!"

Why did people always ask the boys to be leaders first? *She* would brief her siblings, thank you very much. "Violet O'Pinion had the bone-stick. Her mongrel dog stole it from us. This might not even be the real thing. Violet might be setting another trap."

"Sh-she didn't set a trap last time!" Wendell insisted. "Her w-wicked aunt did." Wendell studied the plant for a while, then looked to Mona and Thea. "It's not moving around now. And it's not pulling anymore. That's strange, isn't it?"

"Maybe all the purified air in Violet's room made it move?" Thea suggested.

Or maybe it was all a trick, Mona thought, again. How many times did she need to remind them that *Violet* was an *O'Pinion*?

Sundae gently took the potted plant from Wendell's arms. "Oh my. That one is bigger than the others. Should we . . . uproot it?"

"T-too bad S-Sal's not here," Wendell said. "H-he would kn-know. S-since it's a p-plant."

"Know what?" Sal stood in the doorway of the library, the tools on his sleeves beaded and dripping with rain. Thick mud covered his boots and pants. And he smelled like one of Toot's toots.

"Where've you been?" Mona asked, waving a cluster of flies away from her nose. Why had flies followed him inside? Fiona, Mona's pet Venus flytrap (which Sundae had settled onto the horror section of the bookshelf), began snapping in satisfied delight at all the insects buzzing around.

"None of your business," Sal said, running up beside Wendell and reaching for the plant. But Mona snatched it away before he could take it.

"Sal isn't the only capable thinker in this family," Mona said, plopping the plant on the desk. She pushed the dirt away to pull the bone-stick free. A strip of thick, dirty paper dangled from the end that had been covered in dirt.

"Gentle!" Sal yelled. "Wait . . . is that a clue?"

Mona grabbed a pair of tweezers from Sal's sleeve and pulled the paper loose. "Tape," she concluded. Odd, she thought.

The children crowded in around Mona, watching as she brushed the rest of the dirt away.

Thea squealed. "That is definitely a bone-stick. It's definitely one of Grandpa's!"

They all looked up at the same time, toward an old painting hanging in the library. The picture showed Grandpa Problim when he was very young, maybe Frida's age. Even then, he had white hair and a mischievous sparkle in his eyes. He was surrounded by his doting parents, plus his six siblings. Like them, Grandpa had been one of a perfect seven. And in Grandpa's hands was what the Problim children initially thought was a white fishing pole. Now they knew it was a picture of the water witch all pieced together.

Of course, the twig from Violet's room was one of his. Mona had known this all along. She kept her voice level; someone had to remain calm in this family. But her heart raced with excitement. "Where are the bones we've collected already?" Mona asked.

Toot puffed a #170,[4] climbed Ichabod, and disappeared from the room, only to reappear with the metal lunch box they'd dug up from the swampy woods—now containing the four twigs the Problims had found so far. Sal unboxed them and laid them gently on the table.

Where the twigs promptly began to twitch. Then click together. Then the clicking became more of a tapping, a plunking. The twigs were like the skeleton fingers of a musician longing to play a piano. They banged a restless rhythm against the table while the Problim children watched, wide-eyed.

"Interesting," Mona mumbled softly, while the rest of her siblings gasped with glee. (Sundae ran for the camera.)

"It's like a family that hasn't seen each other in a long time," Thea observed. "Look at them jumping

---

4 **#170:** The Stinker Retriever: A toot used on the occasion of finding something, whether a missing item or a brother or sister playing hide-and-seek. Smells like pencil shavings and a dog's old chew toy.

up and down, so excited to be together again."

"And look there." Mona pointed. "That's exactly what the new twig was doing in Violet's room!"

The new twig—the longest of the bunch—had stopped clicking. Now it was arching toward the others. Mona reached out to touch it, but Thea grabbed her wrist.

"Don't!" Thea warned. "What if they hurt us?"

Mona nodded. "I don't think they will, but observation is wise. Let's just watch and see."

"S-Sal," Wendell said. "You're the p-plant king. What do we do?"

Sal leaned over to get a closer look at the jumpy twigs. "Let's watch them, for now."

Mona rolled her eyes. That's exactly what she had suggested. Sal was the king of Obnoxious Land, not Plant Land. And not nearly as smart as he pretended to be. The twigs continued their happy dance, rolling and bouncing across the desk, knocking into each other, never connecting. It was as if they were nervous, unsure of what to do.

"Wendell." Mona spoke low enough so only he would hear her. "You should try putting them together."

"M-me?" He pushed his crooked glasses higher

on his nose. "Last t-time I touched one of these, things got w-weird."

Mona smirked. She loved it when things got weird. "Exactly."

"That doesn't make sense," Thea said. "Sal is the plant person."

"Sal is irrelevant to this conversation," Mona insisted.

"Excuse you!" Sal said, whirling at her.

"All I mean is that we're each connected to an element and water is Wendell's." Mona's element was the moon, which she thought was much better. But still. "So I think he could put the water witch together. Understand?"

Wendell's hands hovered over two twigs. Mona saw him swallow nervously and close his eyes. Thea concentrated on her twin as if she was giving him a pep talk in her mind. She probably was. Thump-bump, heartspeak, whatever they called it.

"Ex-xactly!" Wendell shouted suddenly to his twin. Her eyes widened.

Mona sighed. She loved secrets, especially dark and twisty secrets. The twins' secret language was fabulous. But it made eavesdropping so difficult. "Care to explain?"

"We have to d-do it together," Wendell said. "Thea's element is m-magnetism. I'm w-water."

"Magnetism," Sundae explained to Frida, "means that Thea has a special connection to the earth, to metal, to anything that connects together. We also think that's why she's allergic to gravity."

"Yes, yes." Sal waved his hands in excitement. "Enough explaining. Let's try it!"

Simultaneously, Wendell and Thea slapped their hands down on the twigs. And the twigs slammed together like magnets. Bright light beamed from the fault lines of the twigs as they all snapped into place. Wendell gasped, and his eyes went vacant. Thea reached for him. Sundae reached for Thea. Soon they were all holding on to each other—even Mona, who didn't really like to touch or be touched by anyone.

Electric. That's how Mona had felt as soon as Wendell had touched the twigs. Like tiny zings of electricity had shot from her fingertips to her toes.

The library window flung open. The wind roared inside.

Lights flickered, then went out.

Darkness pressed in around them, and Mona felt like she was somewhere else.

On a mountain, staring at a full bright moon overhead. There was a valley down below, rolling right up to the sea. The moon stretched across the waves to a small island of caves. To a woman standing in front of the caves. Mama Problim.

Steeling herself, just like in Mona's dream. Stepping into the darkness. . . .

This time Mona followed, watching Mama slink deeper, down narrow slimy steps.

And then she stopped. Mama Problim's lantern lifted to read scribbles etched into a giant boulder.

Mona's vision tunneled, and the dream—was it a dream?—of Mama faded away.

Sundae was shaking her. "Mona. Mona! Are you all right?"

The room spun back into place. Mona had crumpled onto the floor. Wendell was lying close by. Thea was on her knees beside him, her wild black hair standing nearly straight on her head. Sal sat on the floor with a dazed look on his face, Toot and Ichabod trembling on either side of him. Sundae's hair was windswept across her forehead as she kneeled down in front of Mona. She asked again, "Are you okay, Mo?"

Mona tried to swallow but her throat was scratchy. That last vision had shaken her. It was like Mama Problim was there. So close to her. This time the vision had felt as real as the floorboards beneath her shoes.

As the water witch came closer to completion, her visions were becoming more realistic. Her element—the moon—seemed to have a stronger presence in her dreams too. It was as if the moon was leading her somewhere. Through the woods, along a path to the seashore. Across a silver-tipped ocean to an island of caves . . . where Mama Problim was exploring.

But that couldn't be true. Mama was still on the other side of the world, wasn't she?

"Did any of you imagine you were somewhere else just now?" Mona asked.

They each nodded.

"I saw a w-waterfall," Wendell said. "It was all around me, so full and loud and b-beautiful. Mama Problim was there showing me things."

"Yes!" Mona shouted. "I saw her too. She was down in a cave, looking at some words on a rock. She was . . . in a hurry." A big hurry. Something had been after Mama in Mona's vision. It felt as if she'd been right there behind her, watching.

Sundae cradled the sling around her chest. "I saw the sun sparkling over islands in the oceans while wattabats flew overhead. I was swimming with Mama in the sea."

Sal chewed the inside of his cheek, staring at the ground. "I saw the ground," he said. "Cracked like a garden that hadn't been watered. Then opening up to reveal all kinds of things. Blooming things. Mama was studying each one."

Frida called out from the corner of the room:

"I hugged Mama Problim in my dream.
She was warm and laughing and ready to sing."

They had all seen Mama Problim in their vision. That realization made Mona's stomach feel hollow. "Did anything happen to Toot?"

"H-his fart was particularly rancid," Wendell suggested. (A #1[5] still lingered in the room all around them.)

---

5 **#1:** The I-Want-My-Mommy Fart: Smells like spoiled milk and mashed bananas. Toot's most desperate plea in time of deepest distress.

The words of Mama Problim's lullaby rolled over Mona's heart:

Monday's child is fair of face,
Tuesday's child is full of grace,
Wednesday's child is full of woe,
Thursday's child has far to go,
Friday's child is loving and giving,
Saturday's child works hard for a living,
But the child who's born on the Sabbath day
Is good and wise in every way.
Adventure waits—for good—forever—
for a perfect seven who work together.

The Problims knew they were finding a treasure. Did they need to find Mama Problim too?

"I think we need to talk to Papa Problim," Thea suggested. "About everything."

"No," Mona and Sal said together.

"Grandpa said *we* had to find the treasure," Sal reminded them. "If it's connected to Mama somehow, Papa will only get in the way!"

"Maybe P-Papa's found her already. H-he's on the v-verge of something important, h-he says."

He'd been saying that since he got home, Mona

knew. Papa Problim really had no idea where Mama was. Did he?

"Let's find the last two twigs, find Grandpa's treasure, and then go find Mama," Sal said decidedly. "She's smart. She always takes care of herself."

Sal was absolutely drenched, Mona realized. Had he played in the rain and not invited any of his siblings outside?

"Where have you been tonight?" Mona asked.

"The dump," Sundae chirped proudly. The wattabat in the sling grunted. She cuddled it close and shh'ed it.

Frida explained:

"When the rest of the world gets weary and tired,
that's when Sal gets inspired!
Creative slump?
Head to the dump!"

Toot farted.[6]

"I've missed the stink of the swampy woods lately," Sal explained. "So Sundae suggested I go to

---

6 **#205**: The Frida-plause: Toot's appreciation toot for Frida's rhymes, held politely until she has finished. Smells like fried bologna, with notes of peony.

the dump. The smells remind me of home. And the trash inspires me."

"Too bad you can't enter the art contest!" Thea said. "The one in the corn dog carnival! You could make something from the trash."

The carnival. Mona had briefly pushed the whole carnival hoopla to the back of her brain. But the corn dog carnival was on the seashore. And from the seashore you could see the island of sea caves. Could those be the caverns in her vision? Desdemona *had* been caught trying to get inside them.

Toot clapped his hands and puffed a long, low #79.[7]

"Tomorrow morning, let's have a family meeting and look at the clues," Mona declared. "Tomorrow afternoon, while everyone is at the carnival . . . let's try to get to the Pirates' Caverns. To see if she's there."

The Problims all nodded. It was as good a plan as any.

"Oh no." Thea's voice was filled with dread. She was standing over the desk now, looking at the

---

7 **#79**: The Sleepy Baby: Smells like dirty diaper and sour milk. Means it's time to get the toddler to sleep before a tantrum unfolds.

bone-sticks. "Did anyone else notice the twigs? They came together, a little bit—"

"That's a good thing!" Sal said, jumping up to see.

Frida the Fox pounced up onto the desk and shook her head: no.

"At the twinsies' touch, the twigs did click,
Now all those pieces are a seven stick."

"It's shaped like a seven," Thea said, her chin wobbling. Mona jumped up to see for herself. And she sighed in delight. The twig was beginning to look very much like the water witch Grandpa held in the picture. But it was also, unmistakably, a seven at the moment.

"Something awful is about to happen," Thea mumbled.

"Or something grand," Mona told them.

No doubt, there were dangerous days ahead for the Problim children. And Mona was ready for them. This was her moment. Her bolt-in-the-sky. It was time for Mona Problim to shine, bright as lightning. Bright as the moon.

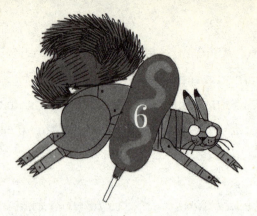

The Mad and Marvelous
Scientist in the Basement

Night pressed in, slashing endless torrents of rain against the windows. The Problems settled in to various end-of-day tasks. Sundae made tiny bow ties for the circus spiders. Toot continued fort-building. Ichabod snoozed. Frida declared she was a fox atop Mount Everest and began to climb the bookshelf. Thea made sure the new stick was far away from anyone who could smash it or, more likely, forget what it was and use it for a fishing pole. All the while, they scoured the rooms and books and nooks for the final bone-sticks.

Eventually, Toot puffed a #27.[8] So Wendell scooped him up and carried him upstairs, Thea following close behind.

Mona cleared her throat. "Papa is in his study, I assume?"

Sundae stopped sewing. Frida stopped climbing. Ichabod jerked awake, crumpling Toot's book fort. They all looked to their oldest sister. Sundae nodded gently. "He had breakfast with me and Frida this morning. He's doing his best to make time for all of us. Then he had one of his brainstorms and ran to the lab. We didn't want to bother him."

When Papa Problim first returned a week ago, he'd had a special backyard dinner with his children. They made lists of all the fun things they would do together, and he'd stayed awake all night catching up with each of them. The Problim parents believed their children were fascinating and inventive, and encouraged them to be curious, always. They loved spending time with them. But for the past few days, Papa had kept to his study for work. Important

---

8 #27: The Once-upon-a-Toot: A fart that occurs when Toot Problim wants to hear a story, or have a book read to him. Smells like musty old books, and one's own armpits after a long hike in the heat.

work. That he must complete alone.

He was trying to contact Mama Problim, they knew. Or at least trying to figure out where she was. And so far, he'd had no luck.

Frida sighed from the top of the room. She was sprawled across one of the bookshelves, like a funny orange frog.

"The fox does miss her father dear.
Sometimes I forget he's even here."

Mona headed to her room in the basement. She'd picked the room down there because it reminded her of a damp, dark dungeon. She dreamed of making it a dreary sanctuary of her own, with slime-slick walls and strange odors. Her room wasn't that homey yet. Slime took time to mature and grow. That was fine. Mona had patience for her projects.

As of a few weeks ago, Mona wasn't the only Problim in the basement anymore. When Major Problim returned home to his kids, he immediately set up his laboratory and got back to work. There were two rooms in the basement, and he declared the other one his work zone. Where he kept the door closed. At all times.

This was odd.

Mama and Papa Problim used to keep the door to their lab open, so the children could come inside and see the fine relics they'd discovered for the Queen of Andorra. Now their father asked them not to disturb him. This was odd behavior.

Also odd (and even more sad): he hadn't disturbed them.

The Problim parents used to want some quality time with their entire family as soon as they got home. They swung from grapevines in the swampy woods, studied bugs in the forest, painted galaxies on the ceiling. One time they made little volcanoes and set them up all around the bungalow to kaboom at the same time. Mona put extra sulfur in Sal's so it also accidentally kaboomed a hole in the floor above. They'd turned it into a trapdoor eventually. So many good memories in the swamp.

But there weren't many memories here just yet.

Mona didn't want to disturb her papa—he was working hard, after all. But she missed him. She couldn't help it. She had a hundred things to tell him; they all did. But she had two particular asks on the edge of her tongue.

She leaned against Papa's lab door, listening. She

heard the tinkering of tubes, the clicking of computer keys, the faint sound of Johnny Cash singing on an old record player that Sal had salvaged from the dump as a welcome-home present. The musical choice was important. Cash helped Major Problim think when he had an unusually big challenge.

He's worried about her, Mona thought. Very worried. Even though he wasn't saying it, she knew he was afraid.

Mona pulled a tiny slip of yellow paper from the pocket of her dress. She'd been keeping it since the morning, eager to share it with her papa. She looked around the corridor until she saw a circus spider, scooped it up, and asked it to deliver the important message for her. (Circus spiders are excellent at delivery services.) The paper was filled with Mona's extra-neat handwriting:

> I like you better than
> a congregation of alligators.

She waited. Nearly left. But then the sounds of tinkering stopped, until she could only hear the music. Soon a tiny spider crawled out from underneath the door, carrying a newly ripped slip of paper in its fuzzy grip. This messy handwriting belonged to Major:

> I like you better than
> a leap of leopards.

Mona smirked. It was a game they played, collecting family names for all sorts of animals. A murder of crows was Mona's personal favorite. She suggested her siblings call themselves "a murder of Problims" but nobody went for it.

She slipped Major's note into the pocket of her dress. Maybe she should wait until the morning to talk to him. Maybe he was trying to find Mama Problim—right this second. She shouldn't disturb him. She was headed toward her room when she heard the door creak open, and whirled back around at the sound of his voice:

"Mo?" Papa's eyes were shadowed underneath. His hair was frazzled at the edges. "Are you all right?" he asked. "Do you need me?"

Always, answered Mona's heart. But she didn't

say the word out loud. She walked back toward him, close enough to rest in his shadow. She liked shadows of all kinds, but Papa Problim's shadow was her very favorite; so tall and shady. She just wanted to be near him. Mona didn't really like to hug people. Or even be hugged, for that matter. Nearness was enough. But she wished she could at least say something to make him feel better somehow. Less tired. Less worried.

"I didn't mean to bother you. I just wanted to ask you two quick questions. One, where is Mama Problim? And two, do you think I'm cruel? Please be honest about both."

"Cruel? You?" He shook his head. "Not for a second. Come over here beside me." Papa slunk down against the wall and Mona did the same, so she was right next to him. So their arms touched.

"What prompted that question?" he asked.

"Sometimes when I say things to people, I think they misunderstand me. And while I don't worry about what people think—not even a little bit—I don't want to be mean just for the heck of it. It's not like I try to point out flaws in people. But I like to know what people are emotionally capable of withstanding. Maybe that comes off weird."

"Mm-hmm, maybe." Papa nodded thoughtfully. "Here's an idea. Find one good truth about someone, and mention that. See how they react. Maybe someone comes across crabby or snobby at first. Maybe that's how they are even, deep down in their hearts. But maybe not. Give them a chance. Find a trait you admire and mention it. Lead with the good, you know?"

"Hmm." Mona rubbed her thumb across the note he'd given her. "I can try that, I guess. So have you talked to Mama?"

He didn't look away when he answered, but the lines on his face seemed to deepen. "Still no word, I'm afraid."

Mona raised her eyebrows. "Oh?"

"Don't let that worry you," Papa said. "I'm sure I'll hear from her soon. She said she was going on ahead of me. That she had . . . business to attend to. If she's not back in a few days, I'll go track her down."

A slight zing of panic ripped across Mona's heart. Papa had tried to say this offhandedly, like he wasn't worried at all. But she didn't like the thought of him leaving again. What if he got lost too, trying to find Mama? Should she tell him—right now—that Mama had maybe left a message in the caves for them? That she might have something to do with this treasure the twigs were leading them to find?

No. This time it was her mind that told her what to do, and not her heart. The last thing she needed was both parents adventuring around in the Pirates' Caverns with the waters rising. Grandpa said the children could find a treasure—not the parents.

Plus, if Papa left, that meant Desdemona would no doubt try to root the Problems out again. This didn't worry Mona as much; it was fun to toy with the dragon lady. But they were just getting settled here.

"Do you know why she went on ahead of you? Why would she go adventuring without you?" Mona asked.

"It's not adventuring that's got me worried about this trip," Papa Problem sighed, resting his forehead into his hands. "It's the spelunking."

Mona's head snapped up. "What did you say?"

"She went looking for a dangerous treasure." Papa Problem mumbled this mysteriously. "But she reminded me, when she left, that she was fully capable of handling it herself. I know she would not want any of you setting out to find her, if that's what's on your mind. I'll do it, if it comes to that."

Spelunking. That was cave exploration. Mona had planned plenty of spelunking adventures back in the swampy woods. Knowing Mama Problim was doing something similar . . . well, that only confirmed it. Mama was looking for a treasure. *The* treasure. The two were connected, she was sure of it. Find one, find the other.

And she would do it—*they* would do it—before Papa Problim knew they were even gone. Maybe he would always see them as children, but Mona knew she was courageous, fierce like a wolf. Bright like lightning. Tonight, she would form a plan. Tomorrow, she would get her siblings on board.

"I can't wait until she's home," Mona said. "It'll be good to be together again, won't it? Good night, Papa."

"Night, Mo. You really are better than a leap of leopards, you know."

Mona didn't smile, not on the outside. But she felt a smile on the inside—a light and fluttering kind of warmth right in the center of her heart. That's how she said I love you, with animal names. Love didn't seem like a special word to her if it covered so many things. So she'd found her own way to say it.

Her parents understood that about her.

I will find Mama Problim, she promised herself. I can and I will.

Maybe that would be her life motto.

Instead of going straight to her room, Mona snuck back upstairs, and outside. The storm was raging again. Wild wind. Roaring thunder. Lightning beaming in the belly of the clouds. While the rain blew over her face and drenched her hair, Mona howled at the unseen moon. Whatever the treasure was, it had the power to bring Mama home. So she would find it.

Maybe wherever Mama Problim was right now—right this second—she would hear that howl and know that her second-born daughter was still here, still thinking about her, still wild inside her heart.

Chicken Sal

The next day at noon, Mona flung open the front door just as Noah Wong raised his hand to knock. Alabama Timberwhiff stood beside him, and at the sight of Mona, they both leaped backward. She smirked. Mona loved it when her very presence made people take notice.

"Hi, Mona." Noah swallowed and waved nervously. "You look busy."

Mona pushed a stray swath of hair away from her face, and sighed. "I'm plotting. It helps me order my thoughts." The boys looked confused by this at first but shrugged it off.

"Can I help you two with something?" Mona asked.

Toot, who was situated on Mona's hip, sputter-blasted a #213.[9] So trusting, Mona thought. Even without knowing if they were friends or foes, Toot was welcoming the boys inside.

"Oh, gross," Noah laughed as he stepped back into the door frame. "That was great, Toot. High five?"

The baby reached his tiny fist for a bump, then giggled.

"I just wanted to pop over and invite you guys to the carnival!" Noah said. "It starts—"

"TODAY!" Alabama Timberwhiff yelled. He bounced on his toes behind his friend. "In a few hours, we have the opening ceremonies. I never miss them. It's my favorite day of the year."

"You all should come," Noah said. And then he leaned close and gestured toward the gate. "And we wanted to let you know someone is watching you." Noah whispered this very softly. Alabama nodded his head to the left and cleared his throat.

Mona stood on her tippy-toes to glance over

---

9 **#213**: The Welcome Fart: This toot begins with the subtle smell of pineapple but ends on a note of sauerkraut.

Noah's shoulder. Hidden behind one of the bushes was Desdemona O'Pinion, watching the Problim house through binoculars.

Mona rolled her eyes. "She does that all the time. She's a very nosy neighbor."

"And she keeps mumbling," Noah added. "*The winds are changing. The winds are changing.* She's saying it like she's hypnotized."

"Hmm." Mona *had* noticed the storm had grown worse overnight. Especially when the Problims snapped the water witch together. The whole town was muddy and wet because of it. "Well, she can't get much closer. We have traps set if she tries to enter the premises."

"So you guys are coming to the carnival?" Noah asked.

"Not this year, I'm afraid," Mona said. "And now, I must finish plotting a dastardly deed." Several daring deeds, actually. "Thanks for the invite, though." She waved good-bye and closed the door.

Overnight, as Mona designed her elaborate prank, she had ordered her thoughts for the two big missions ahead. Ultimately, Mona believed it was up to her—and her siblings—to find Mama Problim.

Papa had basically confirmed what she already knew: Mama needed help. Her help. Why else would Mona be having these visions? Find the treasure, find Mama Problim. Possibly at the Pirates' Caverns. It was that simple. And that challenging.

Also, they couldn't have Papa leaving to find her so soon after getting back. Both Problim parents gone left the family way too vulnerable—the woman spying in the bushes outside was proof.

Mona ran up the stairs, Toot bouncing on her hip. "Desdemona O'Pinion never gives up, Toot." Mona walked into the room of plants, where she'd been working for hours while she puzzled out their predicament. "I can't help but appreciate her commitment to destruction."

Desdemona won't rest until we're gone, Mona realized. Was that the danger she sensed? Was Desdemona still that much of a threat to her siblings? Even though Papa Problim was home? One thing was for certain—the Problim children, not Papa— had to go find Mama. Pronto.

Toot puffed a #104.[10]

---

10 **#104**: The Questioner: A fart demanding further explanation of a topic. Contains notes of spoiled milk and honeysuckle.

"No, we have not set today's trap for her. Wrangling Ivy will trap Desdemona if she gets anywhere close. This trap is for Sal. So you must be very quiet. And very not-stinky. Okay?"

She'd spent the night plotting a special surprise for her older brother. This morning, she enlisted the toddler, and now they waited in Sal's room of plants. She heard Sal's voice in the kitchen, asking Wendell if they had any snacks.

"When I say go," Mona whispered to her baby brother, "you need to toot the Paul Revere.[11] Sal will come running up here, and then you and I will sit back and watch the show."

Toot clapped, giggled, and waited while Mona finished her last-minute preparations.

"Now!" she whispered to Toot.

The toddler puffed a quick #224[12] and giggled.

"Not the Hansel and Gretel," Mona said gently. "A distress toot."

---

11 **#6**: The Paul Revere: A trumpetous fart of warning. One toot if by land. Two toots if by sea. Smells of cruciferous vegetables.

12 **#224**: The Hansel and Gretel: A trail of toots most often used in games of hide-and-seek with Toot's siblings, to help them find him quickly. Smells like marinara sauce and mildew.

Toot squeezed his eyes shut, curled his tiny hands into fists, and tooted the most rank rendition of a #6 that Mona had ever smelled. Just as she had planned, Sal came running. She heard his gardening tools clattering together as he bounded up the stairs.

Sal kicked open the door to the room of plants. "Toot!" he yelled, running for the baby.

The night before, Mona had sawed a circle into the floorboards. She'd replaced the missing boards with mega-bounce trampoline material which Sal now ran onto, unknowingly—perfectly—and went soaring through the air. Everything seemed to happen in slow motion after that:

Sal passed over their heads, clawing for air. Toot waved bye-bye.

Mona pulled a cord connected to a bucket of sticky dish soap, which squirted all over her flying brother. She spun around to raise the shades and the window glass.

As Sal flew through the open window, he tripped a wire connected to a net of feathers. The feathers fell over him in a blizzard of white, and stuck. He burst through the window looking like an angry chicken, which was what Mona had envisioned all along.

She waved at him from the window, a beautiful but sinister grin stitching across her face.

"You'll pay for this!" Sal shouted as a twist of Wrangling Ivy shot off the roof, wrapped around his ankle, and caught him midair. He was stuck for a moment. Long enough for the droves of people walking past the house toward the carnival to wonder why—*why*—Sal Problim was dressed as a chicken, bungee jumping from his house.

"Eu-EUREKA!" Wendell shouted from the room of constellations.

"Problims, pile up!" Thea hollered into the corridor. "Wendell found something."

"Better hurry, Sal," Mona shouted out the window. "Your brother needs you."

Sundae peeked her head out of the first-floor window. "What's going on up there? Oh! Sal! That's adorable! Were you trying to fly? Hold on right there. I want to take a picture of you for the family scrapbook. . . ."

Sal didn't speak. He remained still, arms crossed over his chest, grimace on his face, as the ivy slowly pulled him back inside.

Toot puffed a #133.[13]

"Suit yourself," Mona said with an indifferent sniff.

As Mona walked out of the room, Frida ran up the stairs, nearly knocking Mona over.

"Quickly,
quickly,
come look! Come see!
Wendell's found an answer
to the puzzle that we seek!"

---

13 #133: The Brotherly Love: A toot puffed on the occasion when Toot wants one of his brothers, or will wait for one of his brothers, or just wants to share his love for his brothers. Smells like a grilled cheese sandwich dunked in pickle juice.

The Dreamer's Sights

The Problim children—plus one angry chicken—
sat in a circle in the room of constellations. The
long, seven-shaped water witch rested in the middle
of their circle. All pets were present as well. Ichabod
sat beside Sal, sniffing the boy's feathers. Mona kept
her flytrap, Fiona, close to her side, feeding it dead
flies she kept finding all over the house from Sal's
dump trips. Sundae kept her guitar in her lap, just
in case she could convince everyone to sing together
when the meeting was over. She also kept her wattabat, Happy Henry, close even though he was a
ferocious little biter.

"S-so this is w-what h-happened," Wendell said.

When he got excited, his stutter was extra pro-
nounced. Mona didn't mind; none of the siblings did.
She appreciated that Wendell usually got straight to
the point on a topic. "I l-looked at the c-clue again.
Thea and I b-brainstormed."

Thea unrolled a large piece of paper, where the
Problims had typed up the full clue—along with
their brainstorms.

You've found the first, ←
but you're not through!
There's plenty of work still left to do.

Found in the lunch box in
the swampy woods.

Seven pieces you shall find
And seven hearts will be aligned.
Mr. Biv will show the way,
Where widows watch is where he stays.

Nestled there inside the beast, ←
Is the first clue for which you seek.

Found inside LeRoy the Gargoyle
by Thea.

Mr. De Léon was right to dream,
But no treasure is ever what it seems.
Two lie where all adventures start.
The place where Wendell leaves his heart.

First found when Desdemona tried to
steal it from the library. Was in a book.
Other one is in a book? Which book?

Another's hidden in plain sight,
knock and look — you'll see I'm right!

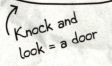

Knock and
look = a door

- knock on every door in town
- knock on every doggy door in town
- checked revolving door at bank,
  got stuck.

A small one in a darkened nook
might require a second look.

✓ Found by Mona on her
personal explorations.

The last is in the dreamer's sights,

What is a dreamer's sights?!

But it's up to you to make this right.
The witch will help, but you must lead,
Together you have all you need.

Mona nodded. Sal pulled a feather out of his nose. "Which one were you working on?"

"The place where Wendell leaves his heart!" Thea said, hoisting up a battered book for everyone to see. "Grandpa and Wendell had a number one favorite book they read together. It was *Tuck Everlasting* by Natalie Babbitt, which we found in this very room." (A wonderful choice, Mona conceded.) "And look!"

They all crowded closer to see a piece of flapping duct tape on the inside cover. The tape looked like it had been molded to one of the twigs at some point.

"There was tape on Violet's twig!" Mona yelled, reaching for the water witch. Her siblings hollered as she grabbed it, but nothing happened.

"We all have to be touching each other for the world to go crazy," Mona reminded them. "Weren't you paying attention?" She showed them the dangling tape on the edge of the water witch.

"So that's the one Biscuit found and took to Violet!" Sal yelled, as if he'd been the one to solve this problem.

The Problems all cheered.

"That's only two more!" Thea said with a squeal.

"Two more and we're on our way to treasure!"

"And to Mama," Mona said.

Sal spat a feather out of his mouth. "I still think maybe we're having visions of Mama because we miss her."

Mona was growing frustrated now. "What other treasure would she be looking for? I think the moon tells me things. The moon is telling me that when we finally get there—to those caverns—Mama will be there waiting."

"Or!" Sundae said excitedly. "You saw a full moon in your vision, Mona. The moon will be full on Saturday. Maybe that's when she'll be there?"

Mona considered this. It was a good thought.

"We'll need the water witch to find our way through the caverns to what we're looking for," Sal said. He pulled a pair of pliers off one of his sleeves and banged it on the floor like a gavel. "Problims, pile up! Let's rally and do this! Two more twigs." Sal slowly turned his feathered head toward Mona. "Show me the clue."

"You should stop bossing me around," Mona said as she shoved the paper toward him. "Our family is a democracy!"

They all quieted for a moment, mumbling possibilities and working through the problem in their heads. Knock and look. The dreamer's sights. What did it mean? Mona felt a familiar joy sparkling inside of her. There were infinite possibilities for how to solve a problem—she loved that part of brainstorming. Sorting through options. Racing toward a conclusion. Finding a new approach.

Thea pulled her knees up to her chest. "There are houses in town we haven't knocked on. We could split up and finish pretty quick. Rule those out, at least."

"We've knocked on doors all week," Mona said, rising to go to the window. She watched people—so many people—walking the streets toward the sea. "It's probably something more obvious than we realize. And the dreamer's sights. What did Grandpa mean by that?"

She flinched when a sparkle outside caught her eye. It was the purple-tailed squirrel they'd met so long ago in the swampy woods. "Where've you been?" Mona asked quietly.

The squirrel was on top of the giant fountain out on Main Street. A statue of Ponce de Léon rose from the center of the fountain; a spyglass extended from the explorer's eye. The squirrel was stretched out on top of this spyglass, basking in a sunbeam. One single, stray streak of light from the ever-hidden sun shone down on its silver chest and beamed at the Problim house. It was almost as if the squirrel—or the sun—was trying to tell her something.

If only I could get inside its funny little head, she thought. If only I could speak squirrel.

"Sundae," Mona called for her sister. "Do you speak squirrel?"

Sundae shook her head sadly. "Glory, no! It's a very detailed and complicated language. That said, I believe love is a universal language for all animals and—"

"Never mind," Mona said, cutting her sister off from a very long glory speech. She was so close to solving something!

Frida pounced up beside Mona at the window.

"I do an impression
Of Ponce de Léon.
If you'd like to hear it,
I'm glad to go on."

"Maybe later," Mona said softly, still puzzling things out in her mind. Still watching that funny squirrel.

"I want to hear it!" Sundae told Frida.

"Hold and hark!" Frida shouted.

"What's this I see!
The treasure of forever,
'tis meant for me!"

She spun around the room in circles.

"I am the dreamer,
I'm here to explore!
I've found a few treasures
but I'm hungry for more!"

Frida pulled a spyglass from the front of her overalls. Where did she get that? Mona wondered.

The fox perched on the windowsill. And pointed the spyglass at Mona:

"You are the dreamer,
if you want to be.

Look again, Mona.
What do you see?"

The statue. Mona saw the statue, holding the spyglass.

The dreamer's sights.

One is in the dreamer's sights.

"It's in the telescope," Mona mumbled softly. Sal had left his rappelling gear in the corner of the room. She grabbed it and bolted out the door.

"Where are you going?" Sundae yelled behind her. "This is a family meeting!"

Thea and Wendell were up in a jump, running behind her.

"Don't follow her," Sal shouted. "It's a trap! Remember the time we all followed her out the door of the old bungalow? She had a whole army of baby alligators waiting for us!"

"A congregation of alligators," Mona mumbled as she slid down the banister and ran back out into the rain. Toward the fountain. She splashed through to the center of it, looped the gear around Ponce de Léon, and ascended.

Her siblings ran out the door shortly after that.

"What's she doing?" Thea asked.

"N-need h-help, Mo?" Wendell called out to her.

"I've almost got it!" Mona said, climbing higher. Her sneaker lost grip on the slippery stone. Finally, she was face-to-face with Mr. de Léon. She wrapped her legs around the spyglass and scooted to the very edge, feeling until she found a hollowed-out spot.

"Ouch," Mona said when her fingertips traced something sharp. She felt again—something loose in the spyglass, sharp at the edge, smooth on top. . . .

Mona ground her fingernails into the stone, trying to get it loose. Just as she had it in her hands, both legs slipped. She spun upside down, legs dangling. She gripped the spyglass with achy fingers.

"Careful, Mo!" Sundae called out to her.

Mona realized that falling from this height into a concrete fountain would not be ideal. She also realized she was stuck. *This* was a fun predicament.

"The stone was slick,
the stone is thick,
but the fox is here to do a trick!"

"Frida?" Mona saw Frida scamper through the fountain; a bright orange streak. Then Frida climbed the statue, scooted out over the spyglass, and rested her hand on Mona's.

"Don't worry, Mo!" Frida yelled.

"I'll never let you down.
I'll never let you go!"

She was a fine little fox. The very best of them all.

"We're here to catch you if you fall!" Sundae shouted from the edge of the fountain. She waded into the water, holding Happy Henry against her chest. "Did you find something?"

Mona pulled the bone-stick free and tossed it down to her siblings. "I found a *booone*!"

A roar of delight erupted from the seven. Mona jumped down into the water fountain as the rest of them climbed inside. They splashed around cheering and the sky threw confetti drops of silver rain.

"Only one left!" Thea squealed. "Then we can find the treasure and Mama! We are so close, Mo!"

"Wait a second . . . ," Sal said. Mona spun to find him. He was standing on the barrier of the fountain, staring at the house. Mona could tell by the way he was standing—by the way he paused—that he was planning. Or plotting. Or both. Mona jumped up to stand beside him and followed his gaze, all the way to the Problim front door.

Frida jumped up on his other side, so softly she didn't even make a splash.

"Carry on, dreamer,
remember the clue.
We're counting on you
to see something new."

"Our door!" Sal shouted. "We haven't knocked on our own door!"

He was right. The only door in Lost Cove they hadn't knocked on, Mona realized, was House Number Seven on Main Street. They all ran out of the fountain and back to the front door. Mona and Sal stayed outside while everyone else ran in—they wanted eyes on both sides.

Mona nodded to Sal. He banged his fist against the wood.

"Who's there?" Sundae shouted brightly.

Mona rolled her eyes. "Don't open it. Just look."

"S-so s-smart, Sal and Mona!" Wendell said, from the other side. "We n-never thought to kn-knock on our own door! We n-never thought of the s-statue!"

Mona felt a trill of delight at being called smart. That was the highest compliment after being called sinister. Or calculating. Or crafty. Please be here, she thought. But nothing fell out of the sky or emerged from the woodwork.

When Sal raised his fist to knock again, she noticed something unusual. She grabbed his wrist and pointed.

Pressed into the wall beside the door was a 7, the house's number. Mona had seen that plenty of times. What she hadn't realized is that the top part of the 7 was missing. At one time, it had clearly been embedded into the stone, pushed in very deeply.

And now it was gone.

Sal pressed his fingers into the indentation, thinking the same thing she was. They opened the door and showed their siblings.

"That's a s-serious problem, Problims," Wendell reasoned. "How do we find it now if it's g-gone from its h-hiding place?"

"What if it fell off and hit the ground?" Thea asked. "And another neighborhood dog got it? Or what if one of a wattabat used it to build a Flip-Nest?"

"I'll ask the animals," Sundae said. "If they know anything they'll tell me."

"Or what if a dragon lady found it the same day she tried to steal the other one? She was just in the bushes watching," Mona suggested, looking at the house across the street. Desdemona had been there this morning, spying. "Think about it! The twig in Violet's room was reaching for something. Didn't you see how that same twig reached for the other ones once they were all together? The O'Pinions must have it. I suggest we search their house immediately."

Wendell's eyes filled with sorrow. "W-we can't b-barge into their h-house. That's Violet's f-family. At least get her to search, not u-us."

"We don't even know if we can trust Violet," Mona reminded him. "Let's just go to their house and see what we find."

Thea lowered her voice: "Breaking and entering is actually a big deal, Mona. The people in Lost Cove aren't going to get rid of us for Sundae's bumblebee parade or for building human catapults or anything like that, but . . . they might not think it's a good idea to keep us together if we break into someone's house!"

Mona looked confused. "Really, we'd just be visiting and then taking back what's ours. Let's go tonight!"

"An-nother idea," Wendell said softly. "L-let's p-put together what we have and s-see what happens."

Thea nodded. "Grandpa said the witch would help, but we must lead. So maybe it doesn't matter if we have every piece. Let's just try it and see if it does anything! If not, we'll still try to sneak into the Pirates' Caverns. We'll tell Papa we're going to the carnival so he doesn't worry."

Sal shrugged. "He doesn't worry anyway. He doesn't come out of his room."

"Because he worries about Mama," Mona said, looking at the twigs. "And we can help. Find the treasure, find Mama. Let's go!"

⁓

Not ten minutes later, Desdemona—who was hiding in the bushes, again—heard the most glorious noise. A loud crack inside the Problim house. Soon after, another. Bright lights strobed—quickly—from every window. Clouds swirled above the rooftops.

"Almost," she mumbled, smiling.

Carly-Rue snuck up behind her and touched her

arm. "We need to go. Or we'll miss the carnival's opening ceremonies." She frowned at the inky-swirled skies overhead. "What is with this storm?"

"The winds are changing in our favor," Desdemona said with a smile.

The Squirrel's Reprieve

Summer nights are the only magic some people—
or squirrels—will ever experience. And it's a fine
magic, no doubt about that. Twilight is a dependable
dance partner, waltzing through the woods wearing
a gentle breeze, enchanting everything in its path.

People rest.

Animals wake, with eyes that shine in the night
and leathery wings that snap the wind. The sky dims,
hazy then completely dark, like the casting of a spell.
A star pegs the corner of the sky, twinkling, calling
the wish-casters and daydreamers to their windows.
Fireflies wake and wander through the fields and
woods. (It is one of nature's sweetest little miracles:

How can something so small shine like a star?)

Sometime around this magical hour, the purple-tailed squirrel climbed to a high branch in the Bagshaw Forest, to watch over the Problim children. They walked into the forest single-file, Wendell at the helm. Holding the water witch—most of it, at least—as far away from him as possible.

"It's not d-doing anything!" he said. His twin patted his shoulder in comfort.

Maybe it wasn't doing anything yet. But it would, the squirrel knew. They were getting so much closer now.

The squirrel watched the children stumble around in the forest. Watched as a rogue splash of sunshine burst through the trees, touching their faces. Making their shadows grow long behind them. Sundae Problim stopped, and smiled up into the warmth. She reached for the sunbeams as if they were threads she could weave together, hold, and keep. The squirrel understood this longing. It was a lovely sunset indeed. A precious break in a terrible storm. This twilight stirred up a feeling in the Squirrel's heart for which it had no name; a feeling where hope and sadness jumble together.

Despite the light, thunder growled, low and far away.

Far away . . . for now. But always moving closer.

"Come on, Sundae," Sal said. "We have to get going."

The squirrel stood up straight, rigid. Alert. Glanced all around to make sure the children were safe. Because, yes, the witch was nearly complete.

But danger—the greatest danger—still lurked. The squirrel would not leave until all was well. And all was not well. Not even close.

Because, yes, squirrels know that summer nights are magic. But not all magic is good.

Opening Ceremonies
(and a Coup d'Toot)

The Problim children (plus Ichabod) stood at the edge of the woods, which was also the top of a hill. The hill swooped down to meet the shore—where the carnival had been set up. And out on the wrinkled ocean, on a very small island, were the deep caves of local lore: the Pirates' Caverns. Unfortunately, the island was well guarded by plenty of park rangers in boats eating corn dogs.

"They would know if she were there, right?" Thea asked. "They would know if someone was in those caves right now? It has to be the night of the full moon when she'll be there?"

"I'm m-more concerned about how w-we'll get there," Wendell said.

"An epic challenge," Mona admitted. Because the park rangers weren't the only ones blocking the caves and caverns off the shore. There was, of course, a carnival in the way.

"Okay, Problims," Mona said, "let's infiltrate the carnival and figure out how to get to the caves."

"I was going to say that," Sal told her. But Mona paid no attention; she lifted her chin and led her siblings toward the terrible chaos of happiness down below.

The carnival was horribly enchanting. It was dotted along the shoreline, multicolored and sparkling. String lights stretched like spiderwebs across stands selling fresh honey, fruit pies, fried candy bars, and T-shirts. Lines for rides (including one *gloriously* rickety Ferris wheel that looked like it might break off and roll into the ocean) tangled through the crowd. Mona noticed the air—how it smelled like ocean air and rain and burnt caramel. She noted a group of young musicians playing lively music center stage: a red-haired girl plucking a banjo, a boy in a wheelchair sitting next to her playing guitar. If I played music, I would add the notes of a sad cello, Mona thought.

Maybe even a fog machine for ambiance.

Then Mona paused. "What is that thing?" she asked. Behind the musicians, near the back of the stage, was an enormous, gold-sequined tube. The tube had strings attached to it, and was curved in the middle. Like a giant, droopy log. Or piece of macaroni. Or . . .

"Is that s-supposed to be a c-corn dog?" Wendell asked.

Toot farted a #2[14] followed by a trumpeting #124.[15] That's when everyone at the carnival went silent. And stared. So much for sneaking in, Mona realized.

"Oh no," Thea whispered. "It's just like when we moved here. I told you something bad was going to happen."

Even Mona felt a bit uneasy, moving closer to her siblings. The last time they'd strode into a town event like this was when Grandpa's house was about to be

---

14 **#2:** The Hangry Puff: A warning Toot fires to remind his family that if he doesn't eat soon his mood will quickly sour. Smells like takeout food forgotten in a car overnight.

15 **#124:** The Joyful, Joyful: Simple flatulence of happiness. Smells like a week-old bouquet of daisies.

auctioned. That fiasco ended with the town trying to split them up—seven children, seven different continents. That's what Desdemona had threatened.

"Papa's home now," Mona reminded her siblings. "We'll just remind them of that fact if they get any—"

Mona's sentence was drowned out by the cheers of neighborhood kids. Waving. Bouncing. Beaming. Even the adults were smiling at them now. Those same neighborhood children—whom Mona still didn't think could be trusted—were running toward them, greeting them. High fives and hugs were doled out to everyone except Mona, which was completely fine by her.

Mona nudged Thea with her elbow. "See? Nothing to worry about."

Thea laughed nervously.

No, this arrival wasn't like their arrival to town at all. Because now all the other children walked with them, beside them, as if they were part of the Problim family. Noah Wong even had a guitar pick, a paintbrush, and a stick of gum stuck to a band around his arm—kind of like Sal. "I hope you don't mind!" Noah said, his eyes alight with admiration. "I'm not trying to copy your look. I'm just inspired!

I'm so glad you all decided to come!"

Mona rolled her eyes. Sal kept tools on his sleeves—that was efficiency, and nothing more. She couldn't believe Noah Wong had actually dressed up like him on purpose. Sal would let that go to his head, for sure.

"Hey, Mo," said LeeLee, their least annoying neighbor. LeeLee's hair fell in braids around her shoulders. She wore a dress with a pattern of flowers and soccer balls. "How's it going? Are those spider earrings you're wearing? Or are they really spiders in your ears? Either way, awesome." She lowered her voice to a whisper. "Just a heads-up, the O'Pinions are already here. Mama says you have bad blood with those folks."

"We do," Mona said, brightening at the thought of her nemesis close by. "Where are they?"

LeeLee nodded toward the main stage, set up in the center of the carnival grounds.

Desdemona had her hands propped on her hips, a sour scowl on her face. Carly-Rue was wearing a sparkly orange dress—of course—along with the exact same expression as her mother. Just the sight of the enemy made Mona feel energized.

"The sight of them together makes me sick," she

heard Desdemona grumble as the Problim children walked past.

Carly-Rue smirked when she saw Mona, and she straightened her crown.

She was such a snob, that Carly-Rue O'Pinion. So obsessed with her silly crowns and dresses.

Find one good truth about a person, Papa had just told her. But surely he would understand there wasn't much good about Carly-Rue.

Frida danced in a circle around Mona:

"Carly-Rue is a beautiful queen,
what a shame that she's so mean."

"Princess, not queen," Mona corrected. "That crown is ridiculous. She wears it like it's going to give her magical powers. Like she really can banish us to the ends of the earth. It's nothing. She's corn dog royalty. That's it!"

Even as she said this, Mona felt a funny prickling over her heart. Like spiders tap dancing across her chest. Her heart didn't tell her things, like Thea's did. Her heart wasn't full of warm fuzzies, like Sundae's. But Mona Problim liked to think she knew herself pretty well. A strange idea began to weave around inside her: Did she just utterly loathe Carly-Rue? Or . . . was Mona a little jealous? It had been Carly-Rue's mom, not the girl herself, who tried to split up the Problims.

No, Mona reminded herself. Carly-Rue was a jerk. She was obsessed with herself; that was the reason Mona didn't like her. And yet . . . Mona watched her nemesis as tons of little girls all huddled around her, all looking up at her like she was a beacon of hope and light. And that same strange feeling stretched out inside her heart again.

"Hello, everyone!" Sundae squealed, spinning in a circle. "Happy carnival!"

The band stopped, and Mayor Philbert Wordhouse walked out onstage and greeted everyone. The Problim children all cheered for him. Toot tooted a special poof of appreciation.[16] The mayor had been a friend and advocate when the Problims nearly got sent away by the O'Pinions.

"Good evening, neighbors! And welcome to the opening ceremonies for the Lost Cove Corn Dog Carnival. Thank you all for coming out today

---

16 **#32:** The Icon: Tooted in appreciation of a person or animal doing fine things in their community, family, or habitat. Smells like a peanut butter and jelly sandwich dunked in pickle juice.

despite this, uh, strange weather we seem to be having. I'd like to tell you a smidge about the origins of this celebration before we begin. Years ago, the first librarian in this town was the nefarious pirate Olivia the Great and Terrible. One day, while Olivia was out pirating, she invaded a ship she believed was full of gold—only to discover an old pirate, surrounded by thousands of books. He told Olivia that stories were the treasure that changed his life. All it took was one book for her to agree. With her change of heart, Olivia sailed back to Lost Cove and docked her ship, making it the town's first library. And she became the town's first librarian. To this day, the Lost Cove Library is located on a ship, which we keep docked over in the harbor right over there."

"A l-library on a ship," Wendell said. "A fl-floating library!" Wendell began zombie walking toward it. Mona grabbed his hoodie and pulled him back into the group.

"Olivia the Great and Terrible librarian had many famous sayings. But one of the most well-known had to do with longing. *I cast my desires into the sea*, she said once. *And the sea returns them back to me, if they're truly meant to be.* Each year, we honor her

memory by doing the same thing. I have a few help-
ers moving through the crowd now, passing out tiny
slips of paper. Please write a word—a line—something about your own heart's desire on the paper. A
big thanks to Miss Sundae Problim for making sure
these paper strips are biodegradable!"

"They won't harm any wildlife," Sundae said
happily.

Noah Wong's older brother, Alex, passed out
slips of paper closest to the Problims. When he got to
Sundae, his eyes widened. A smile covered his face.
"Hey," he said softly. "Ice Cream Sundae."

Sundae's cheeks flushed red. Mona groaned in
unison with the rest of her younger siblings. Except
Thea, who whispered about how "cute" it was that
Sundae had a crush.

"Wendell and I are going to collect shells on the
shoreline," Thea whispered to Mona and Sal. "And
to get a better look at those caverns. Stay here and
keep an eye on things."

Alex had abandoned handing out slips of paper
for the purpose of flirting with Sundae. They were
busy talking to each other about her wattabat,
Happy Henry. So Mona pulled a slip from the many
she kept in her pocket.

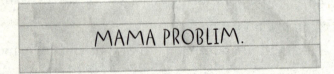

> I like you more than
> an army of caterpillars.

She'd been saving it for Papa Problim, but he would understand. She wanted to write her mother's name on the slip of paper, but she didn't have a pen. It didn't matter; this was just as fitting. Mona did like Mama more than just about anything, and she missed her so fiercely it made her angry sometimes.

"What does *that* mean?" Sal asked.

"It represents my heart's desire," Mona said. "To see an army of caterpillars invade your bed while you sleep at night. What does yours say?"

She glanced at his slip of paper before he could pull it away:

> MAMA PROBLIM.

The same. She glanced all the way down the row, at her siblings' slips of paper. They all had their mama's name on them.

Find the treasure, find Mama. They were so close. Mona could feel it.

"We're getting distracted," Mona said to Sal in a low voice. "How are we getting to the island?"

⤳

Mayor Wordhouse returned to the stage holding his own slip of paper. He lifted it to the wind, where it caught and danced away. "I cast my desires into the sea. And the sea returns them back to me, if they're truly meant to be."

A flurry of papers was lifted high and caught by the ocean breeze.

Upside-down snow, Mona thought.

A confetti parade of words all flying toward the ocean or the sky. Who knows where desires finally rest. But if people had been doing this for so many years, well, there must be a thousand hopes floating in the waters around Lost Cove. She'd never imagined the ocean holding dreams before. It was a more pleasant thought than sharks, she supposed. Though a bit less fun.

"Now our reigning corn dog princess, Miss Carly-Rue O'Pinion, will come up onstage and sing our official town anthem and we will—" The mayor sighed as if he dreaded his next words. "We will raise the

Golden Corn Dog to signal the carnival has begun."

Ichabod *ork-ork*'d angrily. Toot puffed a #217[17] and patted the swine's soft head. Even Sundae stopped talking to Alex and leaned down. "I'm so sorry, Ichabod! They weren't thinking of how offensive it would be. . . ."

"Should we go now?" Sal asked.

"No," Mona smirked. She wanted to stay exactly where she was and watch Carly-Rue O'Pinion make an idiot out of herself.

Carly-Rue walked up on the stage, her flared skirt sparkling in the lights. She waved to the crowds as if she were a royal—a real one!—standing on a balcony in some faraway kingdom addressing her subjects. Mona thought about how lovely it would be if all the seagulls circling overhead rained down bird poops all around her. Alas, the birds did not cooperate. Carly-Rue nodded to the guitar player, who began to strum. She closed her eyes and stomped her cowgirl boot in a loud rhythm and belted out a tune. Her voice wasn't horrible, Mona conceded.

Out of the corner of her eye, Mona saw Toot

---

17 **#217**: The Shockfart: A flatulation of sudden elation, shock, or surprise. Smells like wet dog food mixed with applesauce.

climb upon Ichabod and raise his tiny fist. They rode quietly around the back of the stage, Toot popping little fart-bursts as he bounced along, emitting a faint scent of rotten fruit.[18]

Interesting, Mona thought. A new toot! Was her baby brother doing something nefarious? She slipped excitedly through the crowd to try and see. She walked past Desdemona undetected. The woman was (fake) sobbing, hands clutched over her heart, listening to Carly-Rue croon.

> *Where friends share corn dogs and smiles and*
> *hugs,*
> *Lost Cove! Lost Cove, we pledge our love!*

Carly-Rue's voice was not terrible. But the song was abysmal.

Mona passed Will O'Pinion, Carly-Rue's older brother, who was sitting against the stage with his CosmicMorpho mask over his eyes. She weaved her way past the Donut sisters, then a cackling band of MOOS. (These were the mostly snobby busybodies

---

18 **#40: The Jouster:** A trumpetous rally Toot toots when riding Ichabod. Smells faintly of smoke and rotten fruit.

who formed the Mansion Owners Observation Society of Lost Cove.)

That's what I would call them! Mona thought. A cackle of MOOS.

But where had Toot and Ichabod gone? She whirled around, bumping into LeeLee again. "Having fun yet?" LeeLee asked.

Mona saw no reason not to be completely honest. "I'm already bored. These festivities aren't my cup of tea."

"Mmm," LeeLee said. She nodded up onstage. "It's really her carnival anyway. Being named the Corn Dog Princess is a big deal around here. Sounds crazy, but . . . I thought about entering this year. The winner gets free movie passes for a whole year, which, hello, that's a serious prize! Cooler than seeing the Pirates' Caverns, I think."

Mona stilled. "That's the prize for winning the pageant?"

LeeLee nodded. "That's the prize for every contest. They're really pretty but hecka dangerous, apparently. Remember that soccer team that got stuck in the caves in Thailand? You gotta be careful in a cave. Can't mess with nature."

Mona liked the idea of messing with nature.

"You're sure you go into them if you win? A boat will take you to the island?"

"Oh, for sure." LeeLee nodded. "But I'd rather have movie passes myself. And anyway, it'll be Carly-Rue. She's never lost. And listen to her. She is kinda talented."

Mona saw Desdemona signal to someone behind the stage. Soon, the gigantic, sequined corn dog was lifted into the air behind Carly-Rue.

"Wow," Mona said.

"Yep." LeeLee shook her head. "That's some tacky stuff right there."

Mona leaned to look around the back of the stage. Ichabod and Toot were both chewing on the ropes hoisting up the corn dog. While Mona appreciated Toot's devotion, she knew she should stop them. Someone might get hurt if the corn dog fell, which would not be ideal.

"I think my brother needs my assistance," Mona said brightly.

LeeLee looked at Toot and giggled. "They'll be fine. The Golden Corn Dog is made of Styrofoam. It'll just roll around if it falls."

Even better, Mona thought. She turned to go help Toot, expedite the process. But that infernal piece of advice from Papa Problem surfaced again: find something good in a person. One good thing. She was determined to practice this new skill. That was easy with LeeLee. Mona saw lots of traits in LeeLee that she liked. "LeeLee," Mona called out. "I think you should enter the corn dog spectacle."

"Really?" LeeLee's eyebrows floated to the top of her forehead. "You do?"

"Sure." Mona shrugged. "You have great style. Your soccer talents are impeccable. Why not try?"

"Wow, thank you!" LeeLee said. "You should enter too!"

Mona blinked at LeeLee as if she'd suddenly sprouted three extra heads. "I would rather floss with barbed wire than enter a beauty pageant."

LeeLee laughed. "You might have fun. There's a talent show, a Q&A thing. It's not just about flouncing around in a dress. You get to be onstage for a while. People hear what you have to say."

Hmm, Mona thought. She did like the idea of performing. What wasn't to love about a stage for her to showcase the many talents she possessed? Also, she liked the idea of competing with Carly-Rue. She imagined the look on her face when she knew Mona was entering, and oh . . . *that* seemed dreamy.

Mona had a little advantage in all this corn dog business. She was Monday's child—fair of face.

Mona had always believed her day—Monday—was the worst in the rhyme. Who would want to be fair of face when you could be cunning and smart and fearless? She'd never given it much thought. Nobody looked any prettier than anybody else, really. Everybody looked fine in their own way. But people were *always* telling her what a pretty little girl she was. Surely that would be helpful in a beauty pageant.

"I will consider this," Mona said. "Hold on just a second, LeeLee."

Mona grabbed a small pair of shears from Sal's sleeve and darted around the back of the stage.

She pulled Toot away from the rope, then patted Ichabod on the head. She guided them, quickly, away from the corn dog's projected path of flop.

"Allow me to help with this coup d'toot," Mona said, cataloging the name for Toot's new stink bomb.

Ichabod nuzzled her leg lovingly. (Mona didn't generally like to be touched. She made exceptions for animals. And Toot.)

A quick, loud snap echoed through the carnival grounds when Mona cut the ropes. Carly-Rue stopped singing. The crowd went silent. The corn dog groaned as it fell, slowly, raining glitter and sparkles down all around them. Carly-Rue jumped into the audience with a scream just as the corn dog fell to the stage and began bounce-rolling toward the ocean.

Everyone turned, quietly, and looked at the Problims.

"Smile!" Sundae said, snapping a picture.

"No!" Desdemona shouted, chasing the corn dog down the shore. "COME BACK!" She ran after it, jumped on it as if it were a log-rolling competition, and rode it all the way into the ocean. She held the Golden Corn Dog while it floated, trying to swim it back to shore but mostly getting dunked over and over. "I worked all day on this!"

Sundae snapped a picture for the scrapbook.

Frida took a picture for her heart.

The mayor laughed and raised his hands in delight. "I declare the Seventy-Seventh Annual Lost Cove Corn Dog Carnival open!"

The Problims were cheering so loudly they didn't notice a soaking-wet Desdemona until she was standing right behind them, scowling like a creature from the deep. "Well done, Problims," she growled under her breath. "This time you're done for."

A Firm Decision

Desdemona O'Pinion stood on the front lawn of the Problim house, drenched and shouting. Her voice was so shrill, Mona flinched and covered Toot's ears. The Problim children, their father, and Mayor Wordhouse all waited not so patiently for Desdemona to finish. Somehow, most of the rest of the carnival crowd had ended up in the front yard of the Problim house too. (It's a known rule in small towns: follow the action, or you'll have nothing to do.)

"They are a danger to other children!" Desdemona shouted as she pointed at the Problim children. "Do you know how hard the MOOS worked on the Golden Corn Dog this year? How rude of you, Mona

Problim. How careless and immature of you to ruin Carly-Rue's shining moment! You are cruel."

Ugh, that word again. Mona wasn't cruel! And this time, she didn't have to defend herself.

Major Problim stepped in front of his kids. "If you have an issue, Desdemona, you can speak to me. Leave my children alone." More softly, he added: "When did you become such a bully?"

"Time changes all of us," Desdemona said, pushing a swoop of soggy blond hair from her face. "Clearly, it has made your family even worse than they already were."

Major Problim's children stood in his shadow with confidence. Mona knew no one could hurt them if her dad was there. And they wouldn't let anyone hurt him either. Major cleared his throat and said, "I just want to make sure I understand correctly. You are angry because of . . . a giant corn dog?"

"Yes," Desdemona said. "Each year it drops onto the stage. Like the ball in Times Square."

"But it's *not* the ball in Times Square," Major said softly. "It's a corn dog."

The mayor nodded his agreement.

"It's festive!" Desdemona yelled. "It's tradition."

Now Sal spoke up: "Ichabod was so hurt when

he saw it. If you had a pet pig, you'd understand. It's a little insensitive. Everybody loves Ichabod."

"First of all, he is your pet pig," Desdemona said. "Not the cove's pet pig. Second, I'm not worried about your stinky little brother or your pet swine." She pointed a shaky finger at Mona. "I saw that urchin snip the rope that held the corn dog in place. What if it had hurt someone when it fell?"

"The corn dog is made of foam," Mona said sweetly. "If injury is what you're going for, I would recommend making the next one out of shrapnel or glass—"

Sundae nudged Mona hard in the side.

Desdemona narrowed her eyes. "Thank goodness Mona Problim's not in any competition. I would be afraid for my children's lives."

"Actually, I am in a competition," Mona said, and looked Carly-Rue in the eye. She spoke loud enough for the entire cove to hear. "I'm entering the pageant. I intend to be this year's Corn Dog Princess."

"Really?" Papa Problim and Sal said in unison.

Desdemona's face paled.

Sundae squealed and clapped. "Glory! How fun, Mona!"

Carly-Rue's mouth dropped open. ". . . What?"

Mona narrowed her eyes at Carly-Rue. And Carly-Rue did the same thing. The moment reminded her of a scene in an old Western, the two of them facing off for a colossal showdown. Mona smirked. "You heard me."

"If Mona's in, I'm definitely in," LeeLee said, coming to stand beside her. "If the Problems are down, this is going to be fun."

"I'll enter!" came a soft voice in the crowd. Melody Larson stood with her service dog, Xena. "If LeeLee's in it, then I am too. We'll all have the best time." LeeLee and Melody put their arms around each other's shoulders.

Mona looked at her sisters. "Misery loves company. Don't forget, the winner of each contest gets a boat ride to the Pirates' Caverns. What do you say?"

Wendell reached out and shook her shoulders. "Who are you and what have you d-done to my evil sister?"

Mona smiled. She was elated by the look of shock in their eyes. No one was expecting her to enter this particular competition. But it was perfect. Not only would it get her a spot on the boat into the Pirates' Caverns, it would give her ample opportunities to revenge-prank her greatest nemesis: Carly-Rue O'Pinion.

"I'm so proud of you, Mo," Sundae said. "I will be your standing ovation at every part of the pageant."

"Every *part*?" Mona asked. "There are parts of the pageant?"

Carly-Rue smiled. "The pageant stretches over three nights, with three separate elements."

"Oh. Goody," Mona said with a gulp. What had she just signed up for?

The fox pounced into the middle of her siblings.

"Thea Problim,
how about you?
This would be so fun to do!"

Thea smiled. "I'm not really into pageants. It's fine if you all are, it's just not me. But maybe . . . I'll enter something in the creative writing contest? Something I've written for Midge Lodestar?" Midge Lodestar, aka the Widow Dorrie, was a local radio personality and new family friend. She'd told Thea she could help her cover the corn dog carnival for her radio show. It was the opportunity of a lifetime!

"I'm g-going to b-bake a pie," Wendell said. Mona noticed that he was holding his "fishing rod" so hard his knuckles were white. So far Desdemona hadn't paid much attention to it.

"I'll enter the art contest," Sal said. He nodded to Mona, just slightly. Like they were a team, which felt really nice. Though she'd never admit it.

Frida twirled in a circle and said:

"The fox is a pageant guarantee.
Don't worry, Mona,
it's you and me!"

Sal leaned closer to Mona, his tools clattering together like rain. "Mona—do you realize what you're doing? You hate even the thought of a beauty pageant."

Mona relished the undertone of fear she heard in her brother's voice. He'd made it his life's mission to protect the world from her. Thus, she had made it her life mission to make his life more complicated. "Oh, believe me," she said, "I do."

"I'll enter!" another girl shouted.

"And me!"

"ME TOO!" Alabama Timberwhiff hollered. Everyone turned to look at him. His face flushed. He smiled kindly and laughed. "I mean, I'll be there to cheer you girls on for your pageant. Like every year."

"You are devious," Desdemona said to Mona. Desdemona looked at the mayor. "Mona shouldn't be allowed to participate because of this stunt and you know it."

"Nobody is getting kicked out of the corn dog pageant. I'm sure the Problim children will be a little more cautious from now on. Safety is important for our carnival."

Ugh, that word again, thought Mona. Safety was a practice that kept so many people from living their best lives.

"And besides," the mayor continued, "their father is here to watch over them now. As long as he's here, I know the Problim children will behave."

Mona glanced at her papa. He nodded but said nothing. She hoped he was clearheaded enough to understand what the mayor was saying: Papa had to stay with the Problim children. If he left, they'd be vulnerable.

A loud crack of thunder overhead made several

folks in the crowd scream. Next came the rain, steady for a second before becoming a full-on downpour.

"Everybody be safe going home!" the mayor yelled. "We'll see you all at the carnival tomorrow!"

Desdemona glared at Mona—a look so icy it made all the Problims huddle closer to her. And then the woman's eyes drifted over each of the children, settling on Wendell. On the water witch he'd disguised as a fishing rod. She narrowed her eyes.

Don't hide it from her, Mona pleaded silently. That will make it even more suspicious.

Desdemona smiled, exactly the same way Mona imagined the Cheshire cat smiling in *Alice's Adventures in Wonderland*. "This is odd weather to be fishing, isn't it, Wendell?"

He gulped. "I l-like to be p-prepared."

Mona exchanged a glance with her siblings. It was a rally without any words: a visual promise to look out for each other—*and* their father. Nothing would come between them. Nothing would tear them apart. They would stick together like the bonesticks in the water witch.

"Desdemona." Major's voice was full of authority. "I believe we decided you weren't allowed on my property anymore."

"Of course," she said, turning to walk away. "Because you're not going anywhere, right?" She glanced back once. "You better stay put, Major. For their sake."

Mona hated the wicked lilt of that woman's voice. Low, so only her siblings could hear her, Mona whispered: "Everyone meet me in the backyard at darkest dark tonight for a family meeting. I have an idea."

Elemental Experiments

Lost Cove slept that night, but House Number Seven on Main Street was fully lit and fully alive. As soon as the rain moved out, a low fog settled over the Problim house. Soon, the backyard was strung with multicolored paper lanterns that beamed and blinked. And all seven Problim children met in the backyard at Mona's request.

"I b-brought the book," Wendell said, holding up an old, purple-covered copy for his siblings to see.

The book, *The Seven Ancient Elements*, was written by their grandfather, Frank Cornelius Armadillo Problim. It was where the Problim children had found one of the bone-sticks last week (thanks to

Desdemona, who was trying to steal it at the time). It's also where they got a very important clue about what it meant to be a perfect seven.

Mona took the book from her brother, fingering the pages until she found the drawing she wanted.

"Need a flashlight?" Sundae asked.

"No," Mona said. "I have perfect night vision. It's what I brought you here to talk about, actually . . . here it is!"

Sal did pull a flashlight from his tool belt, so everyone else could see.

Mona pointed to a sketch of a circle with seven different pieces, like a pie. Each piece had a symbol on it: a fire, a wave of water, curlicues meant to represent the air, a magnet, a blooming flower to represent the earth, the sun, and the moon. This same image was also a stained-glass window in the Problim family library.

"You all remember this, don't you?" Mona asked. "According to Grandpa's study, each day of the week is associated with some sort of element. So whatever day a person is born on, well, that's the element they'll have a special connection to. And because we're a perfect seven—that connection is really strong. We all agree that's true?"

The Problems nodded. They'd seen it play out for years, without realizing what was even happening. Sal—Saturday's child—had a knack for growing anything from the earth. Sundae had sunshine in her soul. Thea could make gears shift and turn and open any lock, her special connection to magnetism. Toot definitely had the ability to move air. Wendell, their resident witcher, had a connection to water. Frida could do something with fire (which would be delightful, Mona reasoned). None of them had seen Frida do anything fiery yet, but Mona could hardly wait until the fox realized her potential. Then there was Mona—Monday's child. She was connected to the moon.

"So I have a theory," Mona said. "It's two-parted, really. I think these elements we're connected to, that's how we can find treasures. We manipulate the elements. A perfect seven . . . all together . . . and when we are together, we use these abilities we have to make nature work with us. It's like we have the power to manipulate it."

"And so did the original seven," Sal said, nodding intently as Mona spoke. "That makes sense! Remember how people used to say they thought

Grandpa's family was cursed? And we're cursed, because we're Problims too? Maybe they saw them do something weird with nature."

"And Grandpa knew we could do all of this since we're a seven," Thea said softly. "Grandpa knew about it. He knew somehow it would help us find the treasure."

"Which is how we'll find Mama Problim," Mona said. "That's the second thing. I wonder if—because I'm connected to the moon—my dreams are real sometimes. We all picture Mama when we have our visions. But for me, it's like I'm actually following her deep into a cave. Like there's always more to her story. I think we can find her this way."

"If that's true," Sal said, "do you think she's okay?"

"I don't know," Mona said. "But I feel danger around me when I have the vision. Does that make sense?"

"Not really," Sal said. "But let's try again. Wendell, you hold out the witch. And we'll all hold on to you like we did before."

"It's getting easier to hold it now," Wendell Problim said.

The siblings reached for each other's shoulders, one at a time. Mona was the last to reach for the shoulder beside her. "Ready?" she asked.

Six other nods, and then she clapped her hand on Sal's shoulder and waited. . . . Nothing.

"Uh-oh," Thea said. "Why didn't it work?"

Mona pondered this. "Were we all focused on the same thing? On Mama P?"

Toot puffed The Toot of Intrigue.[19]

Sundae picked him up and nuzzled his face. "Tooty, can you think of Mommy? I think it matters when we all focus on the same thing. Or person."

Toot squeezed his eyes shut tight and the siblings all reached for each other again. Mona clamped her hand down on Sal's shoulder . . . and her vision tunneled.

A dark shore.

Mama in front of the cave, in her work coveralls. Adjusting the pack on her shoulder and walking in, unafraid. My mom is the coolest lady, Mona thought.

Mama, again, holding a lantern in front of the

~~~~~~~~~~~~~~

19 **#200:** The Toot of Intrigue: A faint, lingering aroma that helps Toot concentrate on unusual, yet enticing, bits of information. Smells like old books, cheese, and dust.

cave wall. There was something there—something carved into the rock—and whoosh.

"Ugh," Mona said as she regained her normal vision again. Her siblings were all sitting around her, frazzled.

"Did you feel the ground shake?" Thea asked. "It's like everything went bonkers. . . ."

"L-lightning was s-striking all around us!" Wendell said.

But Sal only asked: "Is she okay? Did you see her again?"

Mona nodded. "She's treasure hunting. But she's in danger. We cannot let Papa Problim go to her before we do."

"If Mama Problim is"—Thea gulped—"hurt, we will definitely need the fountain. It's a fountain of youth, right? It heals things."

"I d-don't know about that," Wendell said. "H-have you not ever read *T-Tuck Everlasting*? A f-fountain of y-youth might not be as g-good as it s-sounds."

"A fountain of youth means you live forever," Sal said. "That you're young forever. Who wouldn't want that? Why wouldn't Grandpa want to share that . . . if that's what it is?"

As Mona considered this, a strange idea popped into her head. "I would only want to live forever if the people I loved got to live forever too. What if there's not enough for them? Or what if you live forever . . . but you don't age physically? Do you really want to be twelve forever?"

Sal shrugged. "I wouldn't mind."

"Or," Thea said, "what if you do age, maybe you live to be hundreds of years old, but you still get sick, and you ache, and you're in so much pain."

Mona nodded. "Would you want to live forever if you just exist?"

Wendell shook his head. "That's b-bleak, M-Mona."

Even Sundae agreed. "That is morbid, Mo."

Mona shrugged. "I'm just saying, maybe the fountain is bad. Maybe that's why Grandpa wanted to destroy it."

"Or maybe it's wonderful," Sal said. "Maybe Grandpa didn't realize how much good it could do. If he had, things might be different. Very different."

After they'd all planned out how to win their contests—plus sneak Toot on board—the Problims called it a night.

Mona walked into the basement wet, bedraggled,

and exhausted from the day's activities. She slunk down beside Papa's now-closed door and sent a note via the spiders:

> *I like you more than a shrewdness of apes.*

She waited, then felt a smile stretch over her face when the door opened and he crouched down beside her on the floor. "I like you more than a sleuth of bears," he told her. "Glad you stopped by here on your way to bed. I wanted to tell you that I'm proud of you, for earlier."

Mona raised her eyebrows. "For entering a beauty pageant?"

He laughed. "For doing something that interests you. Even if it's totally and completely different than your usual hobbies. Or what other people think your hobbies should be."

"Oh." Mona nodded. "Thanks."

Major Problim had never been quiet about how proud he was of his children. He never interfered too much, not unless bodily injury was absolutely imminent. He'd always let them do their own work, then applauded their antics very seriously. Mama was the same way.

It's weird to see him without her there, Mona thought. Mama and Papa Problim: they had always been such a team, each other's very best friends. Mama should be leaned up against his other shoulder. Or outside with Frida right now, counting fireflies and laughing loud enough to scare the wattabats away. Papa without Mama was like a storm minus lightning; the bright, fun part was missing.

Mona cleared her throat. "Here's another one I found today: I like you more than an array of hedgehogs."

"Very nice," he said with a smile. And he stretched his leg long, reached into his pocket, and passed her a wrinkled gum wrapper. "Here. I've been saving this one for a while."

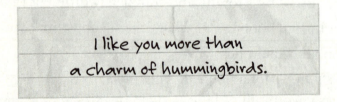

I like you more than
a charm of hummingbirds.

As she read the words, Mona felt a fluttering near her heart, as if there were hummingbirds in her chest all dancing around.

"This is my new favorite," Mona said. She held the slip of paper in her fingers as she talked. "Will you come watch me in the carnival? Even though it's a beauty pageant?"

"Of course." Major smiled. "I'm happy you've all taken to Lost Cove so well. I felt terrible, at first, when I knew this is where you'd ended up. People don't exactly know what to make of us around here."

"Because of the feud," Mona said.

Major nodded. "That's one reason."

"And because they believe Grandpa stole a treasure that could have helped lots of people."

Major raised his eyebrows. "What do you know about all that?"

"Not much," Mona said honestly. "We know that the O'Pinions and the Problims don't get along, but we don't know why. I'm assuming the treasure had something to do with that."

Major nodded. "You shouldn't worry about the why. That feud is old and pointless. Maybe it can finally die out with a new generation coming up. Maybe you can end it."

We're definitely ending it, Mona thought. We're ending it because we're going to find Grandpa's treasure and return it. Well. *Possibly* return it. If it had been gone this long, would anybody really miss it? This was a thought process for another time.

"What about the treasure?" Mona asked. "Do you think Grandpa stole it?"

"No." Major's voice was strong and sure when he was telling the truth. Or what he believed was the truth. "I dig up old relics for a living, Mo. They were all someone's treasure at one time. Now they're dusty, ruined. Nothing worth seeing. Someday that treasure—whatever it was—won't matter to anyone. So don't let people get you wound up about it."

"Are you going after it?" Mona asked softly. "So you can bring Mama back?"

Major didn't answer at first. But after a long, uncomfortable pause, he said, "If I have to. I don't want to leave you. But I have to bring her back. I'm conflicted."

Mona realized her father would probably be very disappointed to find out they were actively trying to find it, at Grandpa's request. She kept that to herself.

"I have another question," Mona said. "Why does Desdemona hate you so much? Because of the feud?"

Major looked up at the ceiling, watching the circus

spiders swing back and forth, playing on their blue webby strings.

"You can just tell me," Mona said. "I can handle the truth of it all."

"The feud was happening even when I was young," Major said. "But that didn't stop me from befriending the O'Pinion kids, secretly. Desdemona was a kid at one time, if you can believe it. We grew up together. And we, um . . . we dated a little bit when we were older."

Not much in life shocked Mona. But this bit of information surely did. Also, it was weird to think there was time when her dad wasn't simply a dad. There was a time he had this whole other life, and that struck her oddly.

"*You* dated Desdemona?"

He nodded. "I think . . . I am pretty certain I broke her heart. And there's a special kind of hate some people have for people who've broken their heart. It's a much longer story than that, but . . . that's the gist of it. Some people never recover from a broken heart."

"Has anyone ever broken your heart, Papa?" Mona asked.

Papa Problim's eyes turned glassy. "I would be

heartbroken if your mother didn't come back."

"Me too," Mona agreed.

He pushed his hands through his shaggy hair. "I'll make sure she does. What Mama Problim would want for you—all of you—is to stay together, and stay safe."

With that, he walked back to his study in the basement, his head low, heart heavy with the thought of breaking. Mona watched as the door clicked shut, as the light in the hallway dimmed to shadow again. She made a promise in her heart that she would bring Mama home, whether the journey was safe or not.

Another O'Pinion

That night, Violet O'Pinion made an important (and secret) observation in her scientific notebook. Then she shrugged out of her wings for bed. She couldn't believe how small she felt without the wings. She'd felt that way all her life, and never realized it. But her wings had taught her that it felt good to take up space in the world.

Violet had always been confined to the tower room—like some lovesick princess in a storybook—because she was allergic to air.

Air!

Within the safety of her own walls, the air was purified. Outside those walls, she could wear the mask her father had invented for her. Her very own bubble-head. But even then, her father, who loved her more than anything, was always so terrified by the thought of her getting hurt. Anything could happen, he said. The world wasn't safe for girls like her.

Violet didn't really feel like the world was safe for anyone. Still, sneaking next door to visit the Problims was as brave as she'd ever gotten. Even then, she felt guilty. Her father would be so hurt, if he knew.

She didn't even sneak into her own house very often, but occasionally, it had to happen. And tonight was an emergency. An Oreo emergency.

Violet kept a Double Stuf stash in her room and ate two of them, every night, before she fell asleep. Tonight, she had run out.

Tonight was also Tuesday: the night she visited a dear old friend. He was her oldest secret. Even the Problim children didn't know everything about her. Violet locked her helmet in place. "You go first, Biscuit," she said to her brave, fuzzy sidekick.

Biscuit swirled around in a circle, then shot through the doggy door air purifier. She bounced down the steps just as Violet stepped into the hallway.

Biscuit scampered through the second floor, then

spun around and wiggled her tail—twice to the left. Coast clear.

Violet scampered past the open doors of her cousins: Carly-Rue was working on her computer; Violet could see a parade of numbers reflected in the glasses Carly-Rue wore at night. Her cat, Miss Florida 1987, was cuddled up on the desk beside her.

In the next room, Will sat cross-legged in the gaming chair, wearing his CosmicMorpho 2030 mask. He was having a conversation with imaginary aliens about a monster cyborg attack. Violet liked Will, and so did Biscuit. Violet had a hunch Biscuit snuck into his room and cuddled beside him sometimes while he gamed. Tonight, however, Biscuit was on a mission. They moved quietly down the stairs together, into the kitchen.

Empty. Spotless. The O'Pinion house was always neat and shiny. It smelled like lemons, and it was completely . . . boring. There were no Wrangling Ivy plants in the corners of the room, or secret passageways, or funny-looking robotic animals. Violet opened the pantry, reached for an unopened package of Oreos, and stashed it under her arm.

And then she heard the music.

Long, low strains of a sad violin curled through the room. A slight gasp escaped Violet's speakers. Down here, she smelled music. Surely this was just a strange effect of the mask, but it was delightful: lime and oranges and fresh water. She moved toward the source of it. Biscuit chewed on Violet's pajama hems.

"It's *okay*," Violet whispered. A whisper barely resonated through that mask, just sounded like a funny crackle. But off they went, down the stairs, into the basement. Violet sat on the middle step. She listened to the music, over and over, that same lonesome, beautiful strain. Violet closed her eyes and rested her bubble-head against the wall with the softest click. She imagined what music would look like if it could turn into shapes, like birds soaring, like rainbows arching over every perfect memory.

Maybe music is in the air all the time, she thought. Somewhere in the midst of all the toxic words people say and all the bad things that happen, there's music too. Something invisible, and wild, and good.

Biscuit let out a small yelp and Violet realized the music had stopped. She opened her eyes to a tall man in the doorway at the bottom of the steps. His long shadow stretched nearly to her fuzzy slippers. The violin was tucked beneath his arm. "Hello there, darling!"

Violet smiled. "Hey, Grandpa. Care for some company?"

Violet O'Pinion had been kept away from most people, for most of her life. For health purposes, her father assured her. If it were up to him, she wouldn't even interact much with the people in her house. But years before she put paper wings on her back, Violet must have had wings on her heart. She began sneaking out at night—always with her helmet—for Oreos. Her grandfather, who had his own suite in the basement, also loved Oreos. That's how they'd become friends and not just family; they both liked cookies and good conversation.

Violet curled up in his velvet red armchair. He pulled a chair over beside her.

"Seven seconds," Stan told her. "That's how long to dunk an Oreo in milk for the best consistency."

Violet nodded her approval. She'd try it as soon as she got upstairs and could take her mask off. "That's important knowledge," she said.

He nodded. "I don't mess around, where cookies are concerned."

The Problims had declared this man—her grandfather—a villain. But he didn't look like a villain to her.

Yes, his nose was long and hooked. But lots of people have pointy noses. He was a tall man, thin, wearing a fitted blazer and a pair of jeans. He had dark eyes—like hers. And, when he was with Violet, at least—he smiled, often. His downstairs suite was warm, and more homey than the rest of the house. Photos were framed above his fireplace, including one of her—baby Violet in a bubble mask. Surely no villain eats Oreos and has pictures of his grandkids!

He dunked one of the cookies into his teacup. "It's been a couple of weeks since I've seen you, Butterfly. I've missed you. Are you well?"

"My dad doesn't like me to leave," she said honestly. "Or even come downstairs."

"I'm not surprised," Stan said. "What's with that bubble contraption if you can't even get out of the house?"

"Exactly! I've asked him the same question, many times, and he just begs me to stay put and I do. Because I love him."

He smiled at this, and it was a comforting smile.

"We've all made wrong decisions for people we love," he said softly.

"Your music . . . it's so beautiful. I listen to it all the time in my room. It makes me feel like I know your heart, even when I can't come visit. Whether you're happy or sad."

"That's probably true, at least a little bit. I believe everyone has their own song playing deep in their soul. When you hear the music they make, you see a very vulnerable part of their heart. Do you play?"

"I would like to!" Violet said.

"Maybe I can teach you sometime. Come visit me more often! You're a young lady now. Not a baby. You know how to take care of yourself and see to your mask. Be brave. Tell your father that."

"I'm an incredibly brave individual," Violet said. "I just hate the thought of making him angry. Or worse, sad."

He grinned at this, and nodded again. He understood.

"I, um, wanted to tell you something. I wanted to tell you about some new friends I made."

"Oh." Stan raised an eyebrow. "So you do sneak

out a little bit, I take it. Do you go to the playground? I always enjoyed a good swing set, when I was your age."

"I don't go that far," Violet said, twisting her hands around in her lap. "I just go next door, usually. To visit the Problim children. Our new neighbors."

The light in Stan's eyes dimmed. "I see. The Problims . . . they probably don't like me very much. Their grandfather and I had . . . a falling out, you could say."

Violet scratched Biscuit's ears. "Since you mentioned it," Violet said softly. "They do think you're a bit of a . . . you know . . . a bad guy."

Grandpa didn't smile at this. But he didn't look offended either. He set his teacup down on the table. He folded his long fingers in his lap. "Then maybe I should tell you the whole story. And you can decide for yourself who the real villain is."

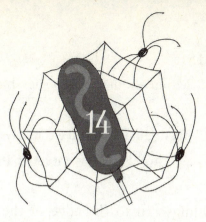

Art Is in the Eye
of the Beholder

Despite the drizzle over Lost Cove, the carnival was packed the next morning. It was Wednesday—Wendell's day—and the first full day of festivities.

"Do you hear that noise?" Mona asked when her siblings were midway through the woods. They'd walked this same path to the carnival yesterday afternoon, but it looked even more disgustingly enchanting in the daylight.

"Hear what?" Sal asked. He was dragging garbage behind him on a sled, so he could set up his art display when they arrived.

THOMB!

"That!" Mona shouted. "Do they have a human catapult?"

"N-no," Wendell answered excitedly. "I kn-know what that is, though! I in-invented it! It's a d-donut cannon."

The siblings ran to the edge of the woods and looked down at the carnival. They saw both Donut sisters, Dorothy and Bertha, sitting astride large cannons on opposite sides of the carnival grounds. With the push of a button, a line of multicolored donuts poofed into the air from each opposing cannon. Kids scrambled to grab a free donut, but were mostly outsmarted by seagulls.

Wendell sighed. "I d-didn't take the b-birds into account."

Sundae draped an arm around his shoulder and squeezed. "That's even better. Imagine how grateful those birds are for a morning snack!"

"Let's try to focus for a second," Mona said, spinning to face her siblings. To her delight, her siblings gathered around her. "Today we all need to enter a contest and, ideally, win it. That way we'll get to go to the Pirates' Caverns together."

Thea frowned. "That's so much pressure, Mona. What if we lose? I've never actually shown anyone my writing before. I don't like to compete. And there are so many talented kids here."

Mona pondered this. "We can sneak you onto the boat. Obviously, we'll be sneaking Toot onto the boat as well." That would be thrilling to plan, Mona thought. Perhaps she could disguise her siblings as wild animals, put them in cages, and insist they were pets who must stay with the Problems at all times! "But it's going to be much easier if you win. No pressure."

"Actually . . ." Sundae picked Toot up, straightening the polka-dot bow tie he'd picked out. "There is a cute baby contest today. That's what Tootykins wants to enter. How could he not win?"

Toot tilted his head at his siblings and smiled, showing off both dimples. He tooted.[20]

Sal nodded. "Nobody else stands a chance." He clapped his hand on Wendell's shoulder. "Are you sure you can keep up with the, *ahem*, fishing rod?

20 **#142**: The Charmer: A toot meant to emphasize Toot's utter adorableness. Smells like baby wipes and sewer gas.

I can carry it, if you want."

"I've g-got this," Wendell said. "G-Grandpa says I'm the w-witcher. I w-want to make him p-proud by t-taking care of it."

Thea smiled at Wendell, communicating silently.

Mona cleared her throat. "Okay, Problims. Let's win some contests and get Mama Problim home. We don't want Papa leaving town to look for her. And we don't want to be at the mercy of Desdemona O'Pinion." Why were parents always so insistent on handling problems by themselves?

A cool wind blew Mona's hair from her face, pulling her attention toward the sea caves in the distance. The island with the crags and caverns was barely visible through the morning mist. Boats still patrolled in a circle all around it . . . but could those boats really see anything on the island? A strange thought settled over Mona, landing like an anchor in her gut.

"Sal." Mona turned to him. "Do you have a spyglass?"

"Always." He pulled one from his sleeve and handed it to her apprehensively. "Don't do anything to it, okay? I'm using it for my art exhibit."

Mona glanced through it, scanning the island, looking . . . looking . . .

"Again, the dreamer," Frida said softly.

"What does she see?
A wild adventure for Sal and me?"

"I don't see anything," Mona said. She looked at them both, biting her lip nervously. "You don't think Mama is in those caves right now, do you? We would feel it, wouldn't we, if she were there already?"

Mona was hoping Sal would answer with an affirmative NO. But . . . he was thinking about it. "She's there at the full moon. You saw it in your dreams. We'll find Mama, then go get the treasure with her. Look at that island, Mo—it's surrounded by little boats. Like Thea said, people would know if someone was there."

But uncertainty kept unraveling her imagination, sending threads of thought in a thousand directions. Mona didn't like the feelings swirling inside her. Sometimes loving someone is the most painful thing in the world, she decided.

She followed her siblings into the carnival while a low storm rolled into the woods.

ulles

Within the first hour, Sundae Problim had won first prize in the public speaking competition with her entry: "Spiders are our friends." Toot Problim won the cute baby contest by a landslide. Wendell went to help out at the donut stands (and work on his Bake-Off recipe). Thea tucked into Midge Lodestar's booth to get some help writing her first creative piece. And Sal began setting up his art at the exhibit ground.

"I can help you," Mona told him.

"Absolutely one thousand percent NO," he informed her. "I don't trust you."

Probably wise, Mona thought. She treated herself to a cone of blueberry donut holes, then meandered around the grounds to check on the carnival happenings. Mayor Wordhouse and Mr. Larson had climbed two tall ladders to hang a banner painted full of pirate ships and bumpy waves.

SEE ANTIQUE BOATS SAIL INTO THE HARBOR! THURSDAY AT SUNRISE!

That was tomorrow, Mona realized. It was too bad the Problems were busy treasure hunting. Commandeering an antique ship would be a delightful excursion!

A few feet away, Alabama Timberwhiff sat on a bench alone. He watched volunteers set up the stage area for the beauty pageant while a cone of ice cream melted down his hand. Such a sad thing to see go to waste. Mona sat down beside him.

Alabama's eyes widened in terror.

"I'm not going to do anything to you," she said.

He nodded, but didn't look convinced. "Last time I saw you, you said you were plotting."

She nodded. "I was. Now I'm wondering. Why do you always just . . . watch the carnival contests? You're so obsessed with the carnival. Why not participate in something?"

"There's a corn dog contest I would love to be part of but . . . the rules say I can't. It's not a big deal."

Clearly, though, it was. He was sitting here thinking about it while perfectly good ice cream puddled around his sneakers.

"Why not just make new rules?" Mona asked.

Alabama didn't respond. Mona didn't know if the look on his face was confusion, or if he was wondering too—maybe he'd never even considered the option.

"Mo," Sal called out, waving her over toward his finished statues. "Come tell me what you think!" (Mona didn't miss Alabama's shoulders relax when she got up to leave.)

In that short amount of time, Sal Problim had all seven of his trash sculptures nearly set up, muttering to himself when the rake on his sleeve knocked over a tin-can version of Baby Toot. He was actually nervous. Sal!

She had to give him credit: these sculptures were cool.

Somehow, he'd mashed all the grossness of the garbage together into what looked like their family. And then, from the trash, he'd set fresh flowers budding and blooming. Mona's face, for example, was a rotten cantaloupe. But her hair was made of full-petaled black violets. It was a masterpiece, completely different than anything else anyone had entered.

"So what do you think?" Sal asked Mona, chest puffed in pride.

She studied each person carefully. Sundae's flowers were yellow. Wendell's were deep blue, the color of water. Thea's hair was made of unruly wildflowers. Find a good truth, Papa Problim had said. But Mona hesitated. Giving a compliment to her brother was hard, though she didn't know why. So she decided to give a half compliment. In the form of criticism: "It's good. I think you should have used more fart blossoms on Toot."

She thought Sal would nod and agree. But he looked livid. "You're a jerk sometimes, Mo."

"What? You asked for my feedback! It's called constructive criticism!"

"No it's not! You're jealous of it. Jealous you can't make something like it." A flash of delight in his eyes as he added: "Just like you're jealous of Carly-Rue O'Pinion."

"I owe her a revenge prank for what she did to us. Besides, she's an O'Pinion."

"You sound like Desdemona right now. Do you realize that? Finding excuses and reasons to keep the feud going."

"*That* is the most absurd thing you've ever said."

"Is it?" Sal asked, keeping his voice low. Which

made him sound even angrier. "Interesting that the people you view as foes are people who are smart as you. As talented as you."

"Exactly," Mona said, equally upset. "It's a privilege to be considered my foe."

Sal smiled, but not kindly. Anytime he lured her into an argument, he grinned that same way. "I consider you inferior, in talent, brilliance, and wit."

Mona was ready to yell back at him when they felt a rumbling over the carnival grounds.

Frida came running from the livestock area, waving her arms at her siblings.

"It's a coup d'toot,[21]
Look out!
Look alive!
The sheep wanted freedom,
And the baby obliged!"

Leading a herd of sheep (most of the sheep had blue ribbons) was Toot Problm, riding Ichabod. He looked like a conquering king, a small one, and he

---

21 #298: The Coup d'Toot: Smells like a horse stable on a humid summer day.

had a determined look on his face as they rode into the woods.

Farmers chased after their sheep. But it was no use, the sheep had flown the coop. Or the pen.

"What do you call a family of sheep?" Mona asked aloud. She turned to Sal but he was standing in silence, staring at what used to be his art piece. The sheep had stampeded directly over it.

"Thanks for ruining this for me."

"I didn't do anything!" Mona shouted. "That was your baby brother! He keeps staging coup d'toots all over the carnival. Haven't you smelled them?"

"I don't mean this mess," Sal said, kicking a rotten banana peel out of the way. "I mean—occasionally—just once, you could be supportive."

"I am supportive!" Mona insisted. She'd thought all sorts of great things. She just hadn't said them. What was the point? Why not just say what would make it better? They had to win these contests or they'd miss the boat!

Sal glared at her, then got back to work rebuilding his family sculpture. Mona—sensing he did not want to be disturbed—went to check on the rest of her siblings.

Say one good thing, Papa had told her. That was

getting easier to do with friends and even strangers. Why was it so hard to do with the people she loved the most?

The judges, who'd seen Sal's sculpture before it fell, declared him the winner of the art contest. Mona considered the day a wild success. They were all winning competitions. They would find a way into the caves, find the last twig, and find Mama Problim—maybe by the weekend! It was almost sad in a way. There was nothing that could possibly go wrong now.

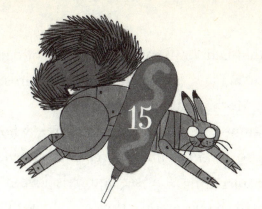

What the Squirrel Saw

The ships came at sunrise.

Mist rolled in billows above the sea. Antique ships sailed through the fog and into the harbor, silent giants dropping anchors all along the bay. All year, the town of Lost Cove awaited the sight of the old boats creeping back close to the shore. This year, however, one creature in town was concerned.

Past the donut shops on Main Street, past a giant old clock tower, past the empty parking lot where the food trucks parked, and past the skate park, sat the oldest church in town—Second Methodist. (Never, ever to be confused with First Methodist. Which was not even first, thank you very much.)

This church had a tall spire with plenty of outcroppings that made a perfect rest stop for birds. And squirrels. Mechanical ones, especially.

Snookums the purple-tailed squirrel, who now belonged to the Problim children, had ascended—first—to watch the sunrise. Squirrels love a good sunrise, a fresh once upon a time every day. (They're very romantic creatures.) Second, Snookums wanted to watch over the Problim family. It had promised this, after all. And finally—after last night's storm—the squirrel wanted to be able to see the pier in hopes nothing new had rolled into town.

Unfortunately . . . something had. That something was actually a someone . . . and he'd been to Lost Cove once before.

He came on a ship that fit in easily with the rest of the boats in the harbor, the kind with sails that billowed in the wind. He disembarked under a cover of heavy rain and walked toward the sidewalk. He was an old man, hunched and holding a cane. White hair poked out from underneath the hat he wore. Like Desdemona O'Pinion, the man wore sunglasses . . . despite the fact that there was no sun to be had.

Waiting for him on the sidewalk was a young girl. She stood tall with black hair pulled into a tight braid behind her head. She wore a jacket drizzled with rain and a strange expression on her face. Not sadness, exactly. She was all business. Soon a cab came and whisked them away to Lost Cove's oldest inn—the Harbor Stone.

As the duo shut the inn door behind them, a wild wind howled through the streets.

Oh, that wind . . . that wild and magical wind.

But this was not good magic the man carried with him. The squirrel jumped from the spire, running for the woods as fast as his metal legs would carry him. The mechanical heart inside his chest pounded out a rhythm: danger, danger, danger, run.

The Spider Queen

Hello! Thea Problim here, reporting live for the *Midge Lodestar Show*! It's the second day of the carnival, which makes tonight the much-anticipated first night of the corn dog pageant. It's been an adventurous week at the carnival so far! Toot Problim and his swine, Ichabod, staged another coop d'toot to free the sheep locked in a pen. And the judges confirmed Sal Problim won the art contest with his sculpture called *Family Trash Heap*. Personally, I liked Frida Problim's entry. She made herself an art installation, which she called *Still Fox*.

Midge Lodestar made the sign to cut. "Press pause," she whispered.

"Ugh. What did I do wrong?"

Midge shook her head. "Nothing. I was just curious . . . which one is Frida?"

"The little one with the fox ears," Thea explained quickly. She went on reporting, despite the odd look of confusion on Midge's face.

So tonight, we have the first installation of the Corn Dog Princess pageant. This is a three-night event, friends. First, we have dress-up night, in which everyone meets the contestants. Tomorrow, we'll have Q&A night. And finally, on Saturday night, each girl will dress in her finest and perform a talent! That's when the new princess will be crowned.

The stage area is more crowded than it has ever been for this contest, most likely because Mona Problim is a contestant. Pageant officials also say they have the largest participation in years. Usually about six girls enter the pageant. This year, we have over thirty. They are all awesome. And they are all my friends. Or they will be before this is all over.

Midge gave her the sign for *wrap it up*. Thea nodded.

We'll be here live, all week, for any shenanigans that go down. And if the Problim children are here . . . you know shenanigans are going to happen.

Because the first night of the pageant was dress-up night, Mona Problim decided to utilize the opportunity to wear a Halloween costume. She had decided to be a stylish vampire. She assumed she'd see all sorts of creative costumes when she walked backstage, but—no. Girls were clustered together in excited, sparkly circles while their moms (plus a few dads) ran around making last-minute adjustments to flowing skirts and sequined tops.

A sharp pain of longing zipped across her heart. She wished Mama Problim was there too. She'd be high-fiving Mona for being true to herself. Or would she? What am I doing in a stupid beauty pageant? Mona wondered. Maybe Mama Problim wouldn't be proud of this at all. And maybe Mona should just nix the whole thing and sneak her siblings over to the caves now. Whose idea was it to make a stupid beauty pageant last three nights? Her mama needed her.

The thought of Mama alone somewhere made Mona so sad that she cleared her throat, mostly to help her think of something else. This made every contestant turn toward her—which wasn't so awful.

Mona was delighted to see no one else had worn a Halloween costume. Even better, she was delighted by their reactions when they realized she had. First, there was silence, as girls nudged each other and pointed.

Then LeeLee shouted, "Yeah, Mona! That's some creativity!"

"I like your clothes too," Mona admitted. LeeLee hadn't worn a dress either. Instead, she had on sparkly black pants and a T-shirt with her initials spelled in red rhinestones. "I like them a lot, actually."

"Oh, thanks! I wish I'd thought of a Halloween costume. Maybe next year."

"Or maybe next year, we should be more specific." The cartoon-mouse voice came from behind Mona. She turned, slowly, to face her very sparkly nemesis.

Carly-Rue looked the way Mona imagined an angry tooth fairy would look. Small. Sequined. Seething. She propped her hands on her hips, glaring at Mona as if she was ruining the entire night already.

"My mother wrote the rules for the pageant," Carly-Rue said. "The rules say formal wear on dress-up night. *You* look great, LeeLee. You look ridiculous, Mona."

"Thank you," Mona said. "You look . . . pink."

"I know," Carly-Rue said. Her skirt floofed out so far, getting close to her would be impossible. Not that Mona wanted be close. It wasn't a bad idea, really—a skirt so huge it kept people away.

"What are you wearing, Mona?" Carly-Rue spat the words.

Mona tried to smile, but that's hard when you're wearing fangs. "Tonight is dress-up night. I've chosen to dress as a stylish vampire."

Mona wore a short black dress, black tights, and black buckle boots. Wearing all black made her stand out just slightly among the pastel-colored girls in line. But what really set her apart were the fangs and red drippy paint she'd drawn on her face, with Sundae's help. Also, Mona carried Fiona, her Venus flytrap, in a glittery black pot to match her ensemble. (Melody Larson was the only other girl with a pet. Xena looked festive too, wearing a collar and leash to match Melody's yellow dress.) LeeLee was explaining Mona's ensemble to Melody; they both laughed and told Mona it was the best idea.

Carly-Rue nearly growled. "It's just that . . . it's tradition. Know what I mean? And you're ruining it. This matters to me, but it's obviously a joke to you."

Find the good truth, Papa had told her. Did this pageant thing really matter to Carly-Rue? Had Mona gone too far making a big deal out of it?

"Fine, don't say anything," Carly-Rue said angrily. "I hope you're happy with yourself. This is still my contest and I'll still win. So, joke's on you and your freak outfit."

There was no good truth, Mona decided. Carly-Rue was a foe, just like Desdemona.

Mona grinned on the inside and looked down into Fiona's leaves—where dozens of small circus spiders waited. "Wake up, little friends," she whispered softly. "Time to take your places." The spiders scrambled down her arms and legs and into unseen areas of the stage.

"What are you up to?" LeeLee asked, stepping in front of Mona, waiting to be called out onstage.

"I'm making tonight more fun," Mona said.

LeeLee nodded nervously, closed her eyes, and took a cleansing breath. She didn't seem to care what Mona was saying or doing; she was just preparing to be onstage. When Mrs. Wong—the pageant's announcer—called her name, she nearly sprinted out to the center, waving as everyone cheered. Each girl was asked to write her own personal bio, including her hobbies, talents, and skills. Mona was proud of her piece, and couldn't wait to hear it read aloud.

"And our next contestant," cooed Mrs. Wong,

"is Miss Mona Problim!"

Mona walked out from backstage with her chin lifted high, holding her Venus flytrap in her arm. She'd decided not to smile at the crowd but to stare—thoughtfully—just to gauge reactions. As she hoped, most people looked completely terrified. (Most people. Sundae looked proud. And Miss Dorrie, watching from the back row, looked amused.)

"She's such a pretty, scary little thing . . . ," she heard a judge whisper.

Pretty, ugh. That word she didn't like at all. Then again, for this particular event, it couldn't hurt.

Sundae and Toot waved excitedly from the front row. Sundae took a picture for the scrapbook.

Mrs. Wong said: "Mona enjoys long walks in lightning storms, poisonous plants, fashion design, event planning, and darkness (the color and the overall mood). She believes each new day holds infinite opportunities for prankability. Her hobbies include playing with her siblings, and also toying with them to see what they are emotionally capable of withstanding."

Mona spun around on the stage and spread her arms wide, as she imagined a stylish vampire might. The crowd applauded. Carly-Rue fumed.

Mona walked to the back of the stage, standing with the other girls who'd already been called out. She glanced up. A tall arch of roses had been built over the stage for the princess contest. Hundreds of spiders were now scurrying around amid the vines and flowers, waiting for a signal to go.

"Next is our reigning champion, Miss Carly-Rue O'Pinion!"

Mona glared at her nemesis as she walked out onto the stage.

. . . And then she felt that horrible stirring down in her gut.

It definitely wasn't guilt over the coming mission. Carly-Rue needed to be put in her place. This feeling was something else. And it magnified when the crowd cheered for Carly-Rue. Desdemona was the only one who had leaped out of her seat to cheer for her daughter. But other people seemed genuinely happy to see her too. Surely they knew the O'Pinions were rotten. That Carly-Rue was a total snob.

"Carly-Rue is an honors student at Lost Cove Middle School," Mrs. Wong said. "She's the founding president of Byte Club, an organization for girls who love to code. She enjoys horseback riding, novels about animals, fashion design, and building epic sandcastles. Her favorite color is glitter."

Mona had to admit it, Carly-Rue sounded . . . okay. She sounded kind of cool, based on that bio. Mona had never had any desire to join a club, but Byte Club sounded interesting. Novels about animals were solid. And fashion design . . . that had been one of Mona's own interests. She imagined Carly-Rue climbing into the trees around her own house—the house right beside Mona's—and sketching new clothes in a spiral-bound notebook, the same as Mona did. (Mona was certain Carly-Rue didn't love to sketch long black dresses and vampire capes, like she did. But the process was probably similar.)

I have something in common with my enemy? Mona thought. This realization made her feel a little queasy. Maybe she should reconsider the mission at hand? No. Absolutely not. She couldn't. She wouldn't. Her eyes drifted over the smiling crowd and that brought back that more comfortable feeling, a rising heat: a little anger mixed with want. A little . . . jealousy?

Was Sal right? Was Mona jealous of Carly-Rue O'Pinion?

The crowd cheered. Even Mona's own family

cheered for her nemesis. The rest of the contestants were starry-eyed, watching Carly-Rue walk across the stage. Why did they like her so much? They just didn't know what she was really like.

The time for payback was at hand.

Mona glanced toward her baby brother, Toot, sitting in the front row with Sundae and Happy Henry. She nodded to him, for he was her comrade. The baby with a plan. He closed his eyes and puffed a silent rally to the circus spiders.[22]

Spiders scurried around the roses and archway, their blue legs flickering like Christmas lights. They were taking their places. They were such efficient plotters, Mona realized.

Mona had already told the spiders what to do. She wasn't as good at training them as Wendell and Thea, perhaps. But spiders were such loyal little creatures. Especially the circus ones.

Carly-Rue came to stand beside Mona, taking her place. And the next contestant was called out onto the stage.

But the announcement was drowned out by the

---

22 **#130**: The Toot of Attack: A flatulation reserved for moments when a plan, or plot, is ready to unfold. Smells like fire, excitement, and a sack of spoiled oranges.

sight of hundreds of circus spiders spinning down from the archway. They appeared to be bungee jumping simultaneously . . . all diving for one person: Carly-Rue O'Pinion.

Perfect, Mona thought. This would teach her to be so rude, so snobby and dismissive.

The spiders swirled their strands of sparkling webs down around the girl, surrounding her like a cage. Mona assumed that would be the highlight of the prank—that one GLORIOUS moment. That Carly-Rue would see the spiders, scream, and run. But she didn't move at all.

Carly-Rue stood still, watching with wide eyes— and a trembling chin—as the spiders spun all around her and began to crawl over her dress. A tear dripped down Carly-Rue's face. She was mumbling something that sounded like, "Please don't hurt me."

The smile disappeared from Mona's face. She felt an uncomfortable coldness around her heart, a sick feeling down in her gut.

"You're fine," she said to Carly-Rue. "They're harmless. They're circus spiders. Just tell them to go away and they will!"

Suddenly Thea Problim ran onto the stage and began whispering directions to the spiders. Some of them crawled onto Thea's outstretched hand. She gently plucked off the others.

"I'm so sorry, Carly-Rue," Thea said. "I don't know how they got over here. You're going to be just fine."

Sundae was there next pushing—no, shoving!—Mona out of the way to put her arm around Carly-Rue. The enemy! Maybe the prank had gone wrong, but now the Problim siblings were comforting an O'Pinion? Carly-Rue would be fine, in minutes. She was probably fake crying for attention.

Mona turned to look at the other contestants . . . and they weren't laughing. They stood huddled together, watching Carly-Rue.

"That's some scary stuff," LeeLee said. "Like, I'm afraid of bees. If a swarm of bees had rushed this stage, I'd be running off or passed out lickety-split."

Mrs. Wong grabbed the mic and said, "We'll resume in half an hour. See everyone then!"

Desdemona leaped onto the stage and swept Carly-Rue into her arms. She wiped her tears away and whispered something against her blond hair. Not only had the plot gone sour, but the fact that Carly-Rue had a mother there to comfort her—even if that mother was Desdemona—made Mona feel cold inside her heart. Lonely, that's what the feeling was. And it was awful. Seeing that affection hurt somehow. Mona's mother wasn't there. Carly-Rue was getting more attention than ever.

Mona looked out in the crowd, imagining their delighted reactions. People had laughed, at first. But now the crowd was quiet. Wendell, Sal, and Toot all looked disappointed as they climbed up on the stage.

"That was cruel, Mona," Sal said, nudging hard into her.

"Watch it!" Mona spat through her plastic fangs. "It was just a prank. The same as we do to each other."

"It's n-not at all the s-same," Wendell said, lifting Toot up onto his hip.

Thea pushed her way past Wendell and spoke in a low voice. "Carly-Rue is afraid of spiders, Mona. Not just afraid, like most people, she seriously has a phobia. Like, you could have really hurt her."

The cold, sick feeling twisted in Mona's belly again. She never wanted to hurt Carly-Rue. She didn't want to hurt anyone. "I didn't mean to do that," she admitted, feeling embarrassed in addition to feeling sad. "I just wanted to put her in her place. She's an O'Pinion—"

"S-so w-what?" Wendell said. "Sh-she has a heart!"

"And it's her mom who's been mean to us," Thea said. "Not her. Not really. What has she done to you that's really mean besides just get on your nerves?"

None of this was working out the way Mona had hoped. She'd thought this night would be fun, and funny. Just a silly joke. She assumed Carly-Rue would retaliate and they'd go back and forth in an endless prank war. This was supposed to be Mona's moment to shine, to prove how clever she was. It was supposed to put Carly-Rue Corn Dog in her place. But it hadn't. And even Mona wasn't amused when she saw Carly-Rue trembling.

She felt like a jerk, actually. Like she was the foe in this story. Like she, Mona Problim, was the villain. And not in a fun, wolfy way.

Mona hugged her flytrap to her chest as the Problims walked home. Rain fell soft in the woods, then steady and hard. Mona didn't pop her hood or her umbrella. She let the rain run over her face, smearing her vampire makeup, then melting it. Only Frida walked beside her. Mona shivered a little, and overheard bits of the conversation ahead.

Thea speaking to Sundae: "Are you upset?"

"I just . . . I never thought she was cruel. I know she likes to play jokes but . . . that was so mean."

"I think there's hope for Mona." Thea pointed to Sundae's hands, which were covered in Band-Aids from all the wattabat bites. "I do. Some creatures bite, when what they really want is to be loved. Eventually, they realize they don't have to bite to get it."

Sundae wrapped her arm around Thea.

Frida reached up and locked her hand through Mona's arm:

"What Thea says is surely true,
There's a beautiful heart inside of you."

Mona didn't say thank you. But she didn't pull away either. She just wanted to get home, to talk to Papa Problim. First, she wanted to make sure he was still there. But second of all, most of all, she wanted him to help her sort through the jumbled-up feelings inside of her.

I like you more than
a cauldron of bats.

NORTHERN PLAINS
PUBLIC LIBRARY
Ault, Colorado

There was one person who always understood her. One person who loved her even when she messed up. The circus spider delivered her message under the closed laboratory door, and Mona waited.

She pulled the plastic fangs from her mouth, and wiped the rest of the smeared, crackly-white makeup from her face.

The spider wriggled out from under the door, holding a square note in its legs:

Mo, I have gone to find your mother. Tell your siblings I will be back. I will bring her with me. No matter what happens, I Lv U, kid. Sorry I'm missing your carnival. No matter what happens to us: Cheer for each other. Stay together. Pile up, my Problims. Conquer the world.

Lv,
Papa P.

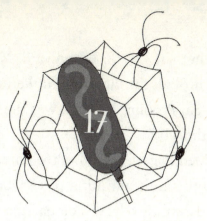

Two Secret Meetings

The Problems were all worried—*terrified*—to discover that Papa Problim had left. Nobody knew where he'd gone, for one thing. Was he trying to get into the Pirates' Caverns? Or did he think Mama was somewhere else? Papa leaving at any moment would have been terrible. But Mona had gone rogue and pulled off a horrible prank that might get them all kicked out of the competitions. Or get people talking, at least. Get Desdemona O'Pinion pounding on their door until she realized the Problims were alone. And vulnerable.

"Something terrible is going to happen," Thea said with a sniffly voice as she and her siblings drank hot cocoa in their still-dark backyard. None of them had slept through the night for all the worry.

Safety, Sal Problim decided, was the most fragile feeling in the world.

He needed to get away from the house. Go somewhere stinky and beautiful; a place where he could make something lovely to combat the blah of the past twenty-four hours. He needed the dump.

Over the past week, the dump had become his private kingdom. He'd shaped trash into twenty-seven different sculptures so far: a ballerina, then an alligator-ballerina, dragons, and bats, and flowers galore.

Rain was falling gently by the time he arrived there, his wagon in tow. He dug through a pile of sweaters that smelled like spoiled milk. "That's what a twenty-three[23] smells like!" Sal said to the purple-tailed squirrel, who had followed him around all morning. The little thing was chattering and clinking, occasionally knocking a mechanical hand against its chest. It was really too bad he

***

23 **#23**: The Old MacTooty: Smells like spoiled milk and sweaters piled in the dump. Always puffed to the tune of "Old MacDonald Had a Farm."

didn't speak Squirrel. Sal made a note of the smell for categorization purposes, then went back to digging.

"Care to go find me some bananas?" Sal asked the creature. "I'm going to re-create the family trash sculpture for our front yard. This time, I'm using rotten banana peels for Mona's hair."

The squirrel hung its small head, as if it was a bit disappointed. But it scampered off just the same.

Sal propped his hands on his belt and surveyed the beauty before him. He was sad to see so many clothes rotting that, once, had been perfectly nice. Why hadn't someone just given them away? Or made them into something else? That's what he would do. He was resourceful.

"Um . . . hello there."

Sal whirled around, his garden tools clinking.

A girl stood before him—about his age, but taller. Girls were always taller. It had never bothered him that his sisters were taller, but this was different somehow. He felt the urge to stand up on his toes, just a little.

He nodded. "Hi."

"Do you . . . live here?" the girl asked. She had

an unusual lilt to her voice. She had a British accent, Sal knew. Whenever Sal read a book, he imagined the narrator had a British voice. But it didn't sound as lovely as hers.

"No. I live on Main Street. I'm here to find art."

The girl smiled, all toothy and warm. "Did you make all this? It's brilliant. I've been taking pictures for days now. I was hoping I'd meet the artist."

Sal cocked his head at her. "Do you live here?"

She shook her head. "No. I'm visiting town for the carnival. I heard about a passel of banjo bees who live here in the dump. They're very rare. They fly so fast that they look like a golden swoop. And when they buzz they sound like—"

"A bunch of banjos playing," Sal finished for her. He smiled back. "I grew up in the Swampy Woods. A hive of banjo bees lives there as well."

"Really?" The girl's eyes sparkled in wonder. "Did you know the rainy weather in the Swampy Woods has changed to sunshine lately? For the first time in ages, there's nothing stopping people from going in and exploring. It's like a hedge of storms used to surround those woods, but not anymore. All the cranky weather's moved into the cove, it seems. I can't wait to see that forest. I'm a born explorer."

Interesting, Sal thought. Of course, he remembered some abysmal weather in the cove. But until this moment, he hadn't realized the timing of it all. A person can't pack weather like you pack a coat or hat or favorite pair of shears. Or could they?

"Excuse me?" the girl said. "Did I say something wrong? You look sad?"

"Oh, no. I'm good. That's just how my face looks."

The girl giggled. "I like the way your face looks! Very thoughtful. A bit pensive, perhaps. So you've seen no banjo bees around here, I suppose?"

His heart felt like it was stuttering when she said those words—*banjo bees*. He'd heard people talk about those bees plenty of times before. They were just words, but the way she said them made him so unexplainably happy. Her voice was as comforting as maple syrup on pancakes.

What is wrong with me? Sal wondered. He cleared his throat. Pushed his hand through his hair.

The girl laughed, like she was nervous. "I shouldn't be bothering you."

"You're not bothering me!" Sal said suddenly. It was so nice to have someone to talk to. Back in the Swampy Woods, all the Problim siblings had wanted to go on adventures with Sal. But now . . . they all wanted to do their own thing. Or they all buddied up with someone else for an adventure. Unfortunately, nobody seemed to like gardening and treasure hunting in the dump. But here was someone interesting to talk to. Someone who appreciated trash. And banjo bees!

And just as suddenly, a mechanical, purple-tailed squirrel came robo-running over a pile of garbage. It barreled toward the girl like it was going to try to tackle her, even though it was barely taller than her ankle.

"What is that?" the girl asked. She didn't sound afraid; she sounded excited. Overjoyed!

Sal grabbed a rusted bucket and plopped it down over the squirrel. "Nothing."

The squirrel banged its fists against the metal, trying to be free.

The girl giggled again. "I'm off to find some bees, then. I did want some pictures of them before I left this place."

"Well . . . maybe I can help you look?"

A wide, lovely gap-toothed grin stretched across the girl's face. "I'm Arianna," the girl said. "My friends call me Ari."

"I'm Sal," he volunteered. "My friends call me . . . Sal."

And she laughed again—one of the most truly fabulous sounds he'd ever heard—as they climbed over a garbage pile to search for hidden treasure.

The squirrel pushed the bucket off his head and watched, sadly, as Sal walked away. The creature pounded its fist against the metal over and over. Seven times—and a pause. Seven times—and a pause. But Sal Problim didn't pay attention.

So the squirrel moved on. There were other Problims who needed its help—who might be more receptive. The squirrel pounced through the trees, away from the dump—and away from the shore—into the forested hills of Lost Cove. Someone was there. Someone who needed it.

The squirrel paused on the branch of an oak tree and looked around. The tree was perched on a high hill. Down in the valley was the place where the river used to be. Now it looked like a deep ditch. A muddy scar.

Sniff.

The squirrel went very still, and listened. Someone was breathing in an odd, mechanical way down below. It was the bubble-headed girl who lived across the street from the Problems. She was shivering in the early morning mist, holding her small, fuzzy dog tight against her chest.

The squirrel scrambled down the tree, pouncing directly in front of her.

Her eyes widened for only a second. And then, shhhhh, she warned. She nodded her head back behind her.

Stanley O'Pinion was there, standing with his back to Violet against a tall tree not ten feet away. He was looking into the woods as if he was waiting for someone. This spot was familiar to him, the squirrel knew. He'd stood in that same place many years before when he was only a boy. Before any of this mess took place.

"You've grown up, Stanley O'Pinion." The voice came from the deep darkness of the woods. It was a strange and weathered old wheeze.

Stan jerked his face toward the sound, adjusting to the early morning light . . . and nearly stepped back in shock. The voice belonged to an old man who had a hat pulled low over his face. But Stan could still see how much he'd aged. And the man still had that rank, vile smell all about him.

"Cheese Breath," Stan mumbled. He cleared his throat, and spoke louder: "Why are you here? You're not welcome in this place."

Cheese Breath laughed, sort of. He made a throaty wheezing sound. "Oh, I've always had a certain fondness for Lost Cove. For the little Problems who used to live here. I watch the weather, always. Always waiting for a break in that magical fog that kept me out. I think this place has something that belongs to me."

"None of this concerns you," Stan said, his voice tangled with anger.

The squirrel paid careful attention to this exchange. But it also watched the girl with wings, Violet, who was usually so brave. This morning, she made herself very small against her own tree, and held her tiny dog very close. The squirrel cuddled against her side, trying to impart its courage. But Violet held a shaky finger against her mouth: shhhhh.

She was afraid of this visitor. *Wise girl*, the squirrel surmised.

"Your daughter reached out to my associates," Cheese Breath breathed. "She said we had a common interest here."

"She's wrong," Stan said. He eyed the man—up and down—as if he couldn't believe what he was seeing. Even Stanley O'Pinion looked young compared to the other man. "If you hurt those children, or get anywhere close to them—"

"Awww, now. Feeling sentimental?" Cheese Breath asked.

"No. I was angry at Frank, not these children. They're harmless."

"That so?" Cheese Breath staggered toward him.

"That fountain belongs, at least in part, to my family," Stan told the man. "You won't scare me into giving any of it away. I'm not a little boy anymore."

Cheese Breath smiled. "We're all scared little boys and girls on the inside, for all our lives. Haven't you realized this yet?"

"This is our feud," Stan said. "Leave. You have no part to play here."

"We'll see about that," Cheese Breath said.

"Trust me, by the time I meet those little Problims, they'll give me exactly what I want. Or they'll gladly take me right to it. I'll have something that belongs to them, you see."

Question, Answer, Accident

Papa Problim still wasn't back home by that night. That's what Mona had hoped would happen. She hoped he would find Mama quickly, then they'd head back home together. She actually hoped she was wrong about Mama being near the treasure. She'd never wanted to be wrong about anything before! She laid awake in bed, with her flytrap close beside her, staring at the moss and mildew growing on her ceiling. Plotting. Planning. Hoping, mostly. But night gave way to another dreary day. And her parents were still gone.

Mona walked onto the carnival grounds that day even more determined to win the Corn Dog

Princess pageant—because she had to get to the caves for both parents. The treasure would get her to Mama. And Papa would be wherever Mama was, she hoped.

Her parents were the almost-only thing she thought about right now. Almost. She also couldn't get Carly-Rue O'Pinion out of her mind. And not because she had more revenge prank ideas. She had to apologize to her. Mona knew this, deep down. What she'd done was stupid and mean. When she arrived at the pageant, she slipped backstage and waited for her opportunity.

Carly-Rue stood in front of the backstage mirror for approximately thirty-seven minutes fixing her hair before Mona couldn't wait any longer.

Carly-Rue was humming to herself when she saw Mona's face in her mirror. She screamed.

"I'm not going to do anything to you. I just wanted to say—"

Tears watered in Carly-Rue's eyes as she spoke. "You're mean, Mona Problim. That's all you are. I won't let you ruin my pageant or my sparkle or—"

"I'm sorry." When Mona said the words, it was like she sucked out the sound in the room with a vacuum cleaner. Carly-Rue stood stunned. Girls standing around chatting and drinking cocoa glanced over their shoulders . . . to see if they'd actually heard what they thought they did.

Mona sighed, and took a baby step closer. "I mean it. I didn't know you were actually afraid of spiders. That was cruel and stupid and, really, it wasn't even fun. I just felt like a jerk. I was a jerk. That was not how a worthy opponent should act." Because there was a good truth in this situation: "And you are a worthy opponent."

Carly-Rue's eyes were big, blue, and blinky as she took this all in. "Um . . . okay. I accept your apology, I guess. I don't want to but I think I'm supposed to."

Mona understood that. "If you ever want to meet one of the circus spiders—in a controlled, loving environment—Thea and Wendell would love to facilitate. Circus spiders actually are very sweet and cuddly. You can teach them tricks. They're the most portable pets. But phobias are nothing to be joked about. Everyone is afraid of something."

"What are you afraid of?" Carly-Rue asked this with a genuine sweetness in her voice. The same way Thea asked questions.

"Conformity," Mona said with a sigh.

Carly-Rue chuckled, just a little.

"I'm probably afraid of a thousand other things too," Mona admitted. "When my parents leave for work, I get a certain feeling—some people call it fear—deep down in my gut. I'm afraid of being split up from my family, from losing them somehow. I'm just in a habit of flipping fear into something else. I don't like to sit in it too long. I don't think that even makes sense."

Carly-Rue nodded. "It does, kind of." She cleared her throat and nodded her head like she was making a resolution inside her brain. Her blond curls bobbed like springs. "I'll consider meeting a spider. Just one." She looked back at her vanity, at all the glittery makeup she had open. "Do you want to borrow some makeup? You look really pale."

At first, Mona thought Carly-Rue was being mean or critical. And even though Mona didn't care that she was pale—she wouldn't care if she were blue—the words stung a little. But Carly-Rue didn't look like she was trying to hurl an insult. Maybe she was trying to find a way to connect, trying to find a good truth.

Mona shook her head. "I don't like wearing makeup. I don't feel like me when I wear it. Doesn't it make you feel fake?"

"No," Carly-Rue said quickly, but not angrily. "It's just art, to me. I love to color and paint and that's how makeup feels. I like my face the way it is, but makeup is just fun, ya know? You wore makeup when you pretended to be a stylish vampire. I wear it because it's fun too." She ran her hands over the glittery sparkles on her dress. "I like to shine. I'm not afraid to admit it."

This quote struck Mona because . . . wasn't that what she wanted too? Deep down, it's kind of why she wanted to join the pageant. She wanted to shine. And she wanted other people to see it. And the thought occurred to her that maybe everybody wanted that sometimes.

"You have your own kind of sparkle," Carly-Rue said, as if she could read her mind. "Kind of a dark sparkle. Sort of an evil gleam."

Mona nodded. That was a start.

Out on the stage the announcer asked a contestant a question: "What would your ideal kind of weather be in Lost Cove?"

The girl thought for a moment. "Tornados," she said finally. "So we could start over and make it better!"

"These questions aren't very inventive," Mona said.

"Agree," said Carly-Rue. "I asked Mom to let me do the questions. I'm more interested in what people are thinking about the world, about what they want to do someday, about whether or not their personal websites are optimized for handheld devices."

Mona raised an eyebrow, waiting for a punch line. But there wasn't one. She had assumed Carly-Rue didn't think about much besides keeping a crown on her head. Maybe she'd been wrong about her in lots of ways.

"Maybe we should just answer the way we want," said Melody Larson as she came to stand behind them. "Regardless of what they ask."

Mona agreed. "That's a very good idea. We'll use whatever questions as a trampoline. Bounce into a different topic. Talk about whatever we like."

It was funny, Mona realized. She was plotting something right now. She wasn't exactly following the rules. Nothing spidery or weird was involved, but it was still fun. It still felt good.

"Up next, Mona Problim!"

Mona walked onto the stage when Mrs. Wong called her name. She saw her family—plus Alabama Timberwhiff and the Widow Dorrie—in the front row clapping madly. Alabama hadn't missed any of the pageant performances. Most people at least checked out the other booths and contests. But he was enthralled with the happenings onstage.

"Mona," Mrs. Wong asked, leaning down to be closer to her level, "what does the word *beautiful* mean to you?"

Ugh. *Beautiful.* Mona disliked that word almost as much as she disliked the word *safe.* Or *moist. Moist* was a terrible word. *Beautiful* was only terrible because of the way it was used. Because it only meant pretty—it had to do with a person's looks. And she thought a person's looks were the least interesting thing about them, always. She'd heard people say "beautiful" plenty since she moved to Lost Cove: they said it about pageant crowns, about nice clothes, big houses, gardens that were neat and tidy and trimmed the same size. But Mona didn't see it that way. So she didn't want that to be her answer.

"Can I think for a second?"

Mrs. Wong nodded. "Take your time."

Beautiful was Sundae with Band-Aids on her hands from wattabat bites. Frida's rhymes and fierce kindness, which—maybe—was a trait as important as cunning. Beautiful was the Donut sisters, laughing side by side with powdered sugar on their shirts—best friends for their entire lives. Beautiful: sleeping in hammocks in the woods, under a starry sky. Mama Problim, digging in the garden, dirt on her hands and light in her eyes when she pulled something out of the ground.

The sadness was suddenly crushing: she missed everything about Mama Problim. Where was she?

"Mona?" Mrs. Wong said, smiling at her. "Have you had time to think of an answer?"

Mona hadn't really. But sometimes it was best not to overthink things. So she nodded, and took the microphone. "Beautiful is the way my mom laughs. She gets these little lines around her smile. A little happiness frame. Beautiful is how my sisters are—all of them—in all kinds of ways. And my brothers too. Boys are beautiful. I don't think beautiful has anything to do with hair or makeup or dresses. I think beautiful is everything you already are, no matter who you are. And when you're doing what you love, I think that's probably when you're the most beautiful."

She shrugged. Maybe it wasn't a great answer. But she felt like she'd said something good, and true. So did everyone watching. They applauded—some cheered—and not because of a prank or catastrophe she'd orchestrated. This was a whole new kind of recognition, when people actually listened to all she had to say. Mona liked that feeling.

A flash from the back of the crowd pulled her attention toward the woods. Mona became laser-focused on a girl in the crowd, a girl in a hoodie, holding a camera over her face.

It was as if the world around her faded to a gentle roar. She focused in on that moment—that one person. I am like the wolf, Mona Problim thought.

For some reason, she couldn't stop staring.

Danger. That's what she felt. Unmistakable—glorious—danger.

All the contestants came out onstage for a final smile and wave, and LeeLee bumped into Mona, changing her focus for less than a second.

When Mona looked again, the girl was gone.

Mayor Wordhouse took the microphone from Mrs. Wong.

"Friends, I have a few announcements to make before we call it a night. If you'll listen closely . . ."

Mona's nose wrinkled. That smell. Like a horse stable on a sunny day. Where was that coming from?

Mona's eyes slid across the front row. Toot was missing. She locked eyes with Sundae and mouthed the words "A coup d'toot?" just as the ground began to rumble.

This could be an issue. Who knows what animal Toot had set loose tonight, but it sounded like a stampede moving toward the stage.

The Problems acted fast. They all jumped on the stage as the mayor was talking, and reached for each other. Mona saw a bunch of baby piglets bound up on the stage (along with Toot and Ichabod). She breathed a sigh of relief. "I think we can defend ourselves against baby swine."

She picked up her brother just as Thea grabbed her other arm.

"NO!" Mona screamed, as her vision tunneled.

And the world turned upside down.

Night Visions

The ground shook, rippling the tall tents set up over the food stands. The arch of flowers above the stage leaned with a low *creeeeak*, teetering toward the crowd. The crowd, seeing this, ran, hands covering heads. A wild wind roared through the carnival grounds. The ocean crashed against the shore. And Mona felt a magnetic pull in her chest. She looked to the sky—it was cloudy, but she knew exactly where the moon was even though she couldn't see it.

The darkness was illuminated.

Everything around her shown in perfect, blinding detail.

Somewhere in the distance she heard screaming,

but it didn't matter. She didn't care. She was happy in the night. She wished she could wrap it around her shoulders like a blanket and fall asleep inside it. The same vision overwhelmed her senses: Mama Problim wandering into a cave, running lower, lower, sloshing through ankle-deep water. Holding a lantern up to read the writing on a flat rock and then . . . hiding something. Something in a nook behind the rock. Mama stepped back and extinguished the light and then, a scream. Something grabbed her mama's shoulder.

"Let go!" It was Sal's voice, somewhere in the distance. She could barely hear it over the wind. "You can control it!"

The hands on either side of Mona turned loose and she fell backward, slamming against the stage, along with the rest of her siblings.

It was like waking up from a dream. She looked around to discover that the entire stage area was a mess. The arch of roses had fallen. The ocean had thrown waves up to the perimeter of the stage. No one looked hurt, but families were all huddled together. Some people were shaking.

LeeLee had run off the stage and into her mom's arms down in the seating area. Mona watched as their eyes grew wide—wider—at something happening behind her. Mona turned to see a massive wave curling above the stage, ready to crash down into the seats.

Wendell bounced up to his feet and pointed at the water. "N-no!" he commanded. The wave dispersed to tiny raindrops, sprinkling down on them.

Mayor Wordhouse scrambled to help the Problim children. "Are you okay, kids? This weather is bonkers."

"Glory! The weather is glorious," Sundae said, standing up, checking to make sure Henry was okay and then helping her siblings off the ground. "I think it's time to go home!"

Sundae shuffled them out of there quick. But Mona didn't miss some of the whispers along the way:

"Did you see what just happened . . ."

"It happened before . . ."

"The other ones could do it too."

"Are they the reason?"

Sal shook his head. "This isn't good."

"We'll discuss when we get home," Sundae said through a strained smile.

Only Mona looked back at the carnival grounds. Most people had run to cars and scrambled home. But Desdemona stood, watching, a smile on her face obvious even from far, far away.

The Problims raced back to their house, locked the door, and ran to the room of constellations. They were windswept, dirty, and a little bit addled from everything that had just happened.

"Someone has Mama," Mona said, spinning to a stop in the front of the room. "She was in the cave. Maybe the Pirates' Caverns. Maybe somewhere else. Someone grabbed her. Did you see the same thing?"

"P-pretty much," Wendell said. One by one, the rest of them nodded.

"Hmm." Mona looked at the baby. "I guess you can't tell me what you saw, Toot?"

He couldn't. But he farted a #220.[24]

"It was just like the other night when Wendell put the sticks together," Thea said. "Toot's toot was . . . ripe."

"And the storm," Mona said, picking her brother

---

24 #220: The Storm Chaser: More dependable than a bad-weather radio, Toot Problim's emergency warning fart for bad (or strange) weather. Smells like wet dog and mildew.

up. "If it's the atmosphere Toot can manipulate when we're all together . . . does he make the storm worse?"

"Do we all make it worse?" Thea asked.

"I think so," Mona said, passing back and forth. "Did you hear what people were saying? They talked about the original seven. Like Grandpa's family could do things too. Maybe that's another reason they were afraid of us for so long. All those rumors of magic had to do with them manipulating weather, maybe. Those stories have just built up all these years. One more night, and we'll all have tickets for the caverns."

"We don't have the last twig!" Sal shouted.

Mona smirked. "I'm on it."

He narrowed his eyes. "What does that mean? You didn't sneak into the O'Pinion house, did you?"

"Not exactly."

"Mona!" Sal shouted. "Did you send in the spiders? Like they won't know that's us?"

"We need the final twig and I know that's where it is. You're only jealous you didn't think of it—"

"Shhh." Thea waved her hands anxiously. She whispered, "Do you hear that?"

A low, scratching sound at the door echoed in the silence.

Wendell slipped the witch behind his back, hiding it.

"What is that?" Thea whispered, fear in her voice.

Another scratch . . . scratch . . . scratch.

"Whatever it is, we stay together," Mona told them. "Just like Mama said. If it's Desdemona, if she tries to split us again, we will not let her."

They didn't huddle together this time; they stood in a line, facing the door. Hands outstretched, ready to connect.

Another low scratch . . . scratch . . . scratch, and then . . .

The Spiders Tell a Tale

The doggy door flapped open and Biscuit O'Pinion pounced into the foyer, shaking the rain loose from her fur. A scroll was attached to her floral collar.

The Problims sighed in relief as Mona reached for the note.

Come quickly!
I discovered something!
Also, YOU ARE IN DANGER LIKE WHOA.
—Violet

Sundae stayed back at the house with Toot and Frida. But four Problems immediately traversed the zip line to Violet's room. Mona was the last to jump through the widow, which was wide-open this time. Violet stood in the middle of the floor, waiting.

She was wearing her wings, but that's not what Mona noticed first. She noticed that Violet wasn't smiling. She looked frustrated. Maybe a little angry as she opened the window.

"You have a serious problem, Problems," she said as they all settled in the room. "There's someone who knows about the fountain. He wants it, and he's going to find a way to make you take him to it. I haven't seen his face but he sounds vicious some-how—"

"Wait!" Mona held up a hand. "Are you talking about Stan?"

"My grandfather?" Violet's eyebrows smooshed angrily. "No. This is a *true* villain. Someone who wants to hurt you. I think there's some history. I think he's come here looking for the fountain before."

"H-how do you kn-know about him?" Wendell asked.

Violet bit her lip, as if she was concentrating

carefully on her words. While the gesture itself was wise, it was also cagey, Mona noted.

"I can't tell you my source," Violet finally said. "Not yet. But I *am* looking out for you. And this villain is bad. Cheese Breath—that's his nickname."

Sal shook his head. "That doesn't sound very fierce."

"It sounds like a Toot scent," Thea observed. "How did you even hear about this Violet?"

"That's all I can tell you about that. For now. Please trust me on this, okay? Just watch your back. He's looking for you. That's the first reason I called you here. But there's another."

Violet's face flickered from worry to frustration in an instant. Or was it anger? And why did Violet O'Pinion have the right to be angry? She was the one holding things back. She was the one who knew things she wouldn't tell them.

"You know where the last twig is," Mona said softly.

Violet gritted her teeth. "The spiders you sent are still looking," she said softly. "I would have looked, if you'd asked me. You don't have to do things behind my back. The spiders, though. They have something to do with why I brought you here. I think, before you find that final piece, you need to know more about the treasure. I decided to get to the bottom of the whole feud between our families and I've discovered some things that you should know. Some things you should see."

Violet gestured to the floor of her room. When Mona looked, she was surprised to discover the most elaborate circus-spiderweb she'd ever seen. It spread over the ground like a picnic blanket. The web had thousands of strains, tightly woven, with their usual icy, pale blue sparkle.

"Make yourselves comfortable," Violet said, inviting them to gather around the edge of the web as if it was a giant movie screen. "And watch this. And remember—it's easy to decide who the villain is in a story if you weren't really there."

"What's that supposed to mean?" Mona asked, plopping down beside her.

"You'll see." Violet opened the door a crack. Violin music filled the room. The spiders scrambled, the lines of the webs trembling as they woke and took their places in this elaborate show. As the music played, the spiders began to dance across it. Mona assumed they would catch rumors—bubbles with moving pictures inside them—like they usually did. But this was different.

Very different.

"Music holds its own sorrows," Violet said. "It tells a story. Until last night, I didn't realize the circus spiders could catch music, tell the stories the music holds on their webs. It's like watching a movie."

Web strands wove into people, homes, a tapestry full of images like nothing the Problim children had seen before. The images were full-color, stretched corner to corner.

Violet sat beside the Problims, like a little astronaut fairy. And she narrated as the spiders began to spin this picture:

"Once upon a time, there were two boys who were dearest friends. Stan and Frank. Frank had white hair, even as a boy, and loved the color purple. He climbed trees seeking adventure. Stan had black hair—but not much of it—and climbed trees to seek the shelter of their arms. They spent their days swimming in the creeks, exploring a forest full of strange animals."

Sal turned to face Violet. "Wait . . . they were friends? Our grandpas were friends?"

"They were," Violet clarified. "Best friends."

Mona thought back to her conversation with Papa, about broken hearts and how badly they hurt. Sometimes forever. If Frank and Stan were friends—which was difficult to believe—heartbreak must have happened. And it must have been terrible.

The spiders spun wattabats with gold-tipped wings onto their web—tall trees, strange birds, and the two boys. One in a purple jacket. One in blue.

Thea looked at Sundae's bat. Then at Violet. "Is that a wattabat? Does this story take place in the Swampy Woods?"

"Why are we even having story time?" Mona asked.

"Because stories connect everything," Violet said, as if this was obvious. "Stories are like an invisible web that connects everything. Yes, they liked the swampy woods. The boys explored everywhere together. They had adventures. And they had secrets."

The spiders wove the boy in purple, hiding something away, while Stan watched.

"And like all boys," Violet continued, "they grew up."

The spiders swung across the tapestry and the

web went white . . . then the two boys were tall.

"Eventually, they even fell in love. They bought homes right beside one another." The tapestry showed a wedding party; the man in purple stood beside his friend. Then vice versa. They stepped into side-by-side houses. The purple-coated man went into the house that was undoubtedly Number Seven Main Street.

Years passed. Both heads of hair turned white. The tall men became more hunched, slower in their stride.

Then the man in the blue coat—Stan—was kneeling beside a bed, head bowed in sorrow.

The violin music in the house soared to a higher tempo. And for the first time that she could remember, Mona wanted to cry at the sound of it. This sounded like pain. It felt like loss.

"The great love of Stan O'Pinion's life was his wife, Clementine. When she first got sick, Stan was terrified. But then he remembered a secret . . . a secret his best friend had told him when they were boys. A secret about what his siblings found once upon a time when they were a perfect seven, all together."

Mona snapped her head to look at her siblings. They all looked at each other. The spiders scrambled too, clearing the pictures from the web until it was white as a sheet. Slowly, they began to weave one image in the center as Violet spoke:

"Your grandfather, Frank Problim, was one of seven siblings, as you know. They were a perfect seven, born for treasure hunting. And when they were young, very young, Frank claimed they found something marvelous: the fountain of youth. A fountain rumored to give eternal life. To heal all diseases. Heaven on earth, they believed. The man who paid them to find it was vile, apparently. And he wanted to do something evil and terrible with it. So, the Problim children—the original seven—found a way to destroy it. Most of it. Except . . . Frank Problim kept two jars full. Just in case. Just to see. He kept them in the town safe along with a special stick that helped them find the way to the fountain of youth all those years ago."

"The water witch," Mona mumbled. That's what the spiders had woven; a Y-shaped, completed dowsing rod. The water witch they were working so hard to piece together.

"Yes," Violet said. "That was the treasure. Two jars of water from the fountain of youth. And a water witch that led to the fountain all those years ago. Stan O'Pinion knew that. And he begged Frank—his best friend—for healing water for his only love, his best friend, his wife. She was dying. And even then, Frank refused."

The web warbled as spiders wove another moving picture: a man in blue was on his knees, begging Frank for help. But Frank refused. No.

A blank slate. And then the spiders began to weave and bounce frantically.

The webby version of Stan O'Pinion pulled something from the vault—a jar. He ran away with it, but Frank found him, chased him. Suddenly they were on a rooftop, fighting. Frank took the jar and threw it off the roof. It crashed on the ground below. Stan lunged for it, but Frank caught him before he fell.

Again, the web went totally white. Blank.

The next scene showed Frank Problim in his purple coat, a jar and a long white stick in his arms, running away. Never looking back.

"My grandpa isn't the villain," Violet said softly. "Yours is. Your grandpa kept that secret, that beautiful secret, for himself. He kept the last of the fountain of youth for his own family. And no one else."

Mona felt furious all over. "Grandpa was not a villain. Your grandpa told you this. How do you know you can trust him?"

"How do *you* know?" Violet yelled so loudly her helmet cracked. "You don't! You can't! At least I heard from someone who was there. Your grandfather—Frank Problim—discovered a miracle. Frank claimed his siblings tried to destroy the fountain itself. But, oh, they knew: deep down, they knew how magical it was. How magical it could be. So he saved a little, just a little—until he could decide what to do with it. The town flourished as long as that jar was in the vault."

Violet held up a hand to pause the story. "Now, they might have flourished just the same without it. But they thought the town was special because of this mystical treasure. What you believe shapes everything, doesn't it? Whether or not it's true? Anyway!"

Violet waved her hand back toward the story web. "When Frank's best friend—Stan O'Pinion—asked for just a little bit, a spoonful from one jar, to save the life of someone he loved, Frank Problim told him no. He kept the treasure for himself and hid it so his family could keep it for themselves. That is wicked."

Tears dripped down Violet's face, fogging up her helmet. "What if . . ." Violet gulped. "I mean, what if I didn't have to wear a bubble on my head outside? What if the stuff in that jar saves people?"

Mama Problim, Mona thought. They were all thinking it, Mona could tell, because they were all silent. And silence was not a Problim family trait. If Violet was telling the truth—if the spiders were weaving the truth—yes, it was so selfish to keep something like that. But what if they had it? What if they could keep her safe?

"Grandpa wouldn't do that," Mona said. "I remember him. He was kind."

"So is my grandfather!" Violet sniffled. Biscuit ran toward her, wiggling her tail, bouncing up into her arms. "That's why our family's feuded for so long. Because your grandfather took something—hid something—that could have saved my grandmother's life. Can you blame them all for being mad? Maybe my family is full of villains. But maybe yours is too."

❧

Back at the Problim house, the night closed in around them and made them all feel somber, strange. They were part of Grandpa's weird legacy, the good and the bad. This seven had unusual abilities, just like his seven siblings had. There was no doubt in their minds about that. This seven could find the treasure, and smash it—just like Grandpa suggested. But should they smash it?

Was he a villain? Were they destroying something that could help people they love? What if it really could save people?

How do you know if you are the villain or the hero in a story? Mona wondered. And which one was she?

"Why didn't he just smash the jars?" Sal said, after a long pause. "If they're so bad, if that's all that was left, why didn't he break them?"

"He experimented with them," Mona reminded him. "He thought maybe he could extract the good and take out the bad."

"But once he realized they were bad," Sal said, "why not just get rid of them both instead of hiding another jar for us to find?"

Mona nodded. "That's a good point."

She noticed Wendell and Thea staring at each other intently. "Tell them," Thea said.

"Tell us what?" Mona demanded.

"I've s-seen m-more than w-waterfalls in my vision," Wendell said. "I d-don't think we're looking for a j-jar."

"There's another fountain," Thea said. "That's what Grandpa is sending us to destroy."

Surprise Guests

Throughout the next day, the Problim children lay low. They didn't attend the daytime festivities for the carnival. They didn't go outside and play on the human catapult, or make mud angels. They waited inside, behind locked doors, while storms raged all around them. Together, they prepared for the night ahead.

Backpacks were stuffed full of necessary supplies and snacks. Whether or not they all won a spot on the boat to the Pirates' Caverns, they had to find a way to get there. And there was no telling if they could come back home for a while. Desdemona might be a bit distracted for today, with the pageant coming to an end. But tomorrow, she would only have the Problems to focus on again.

Plus, Violet's new warning: Cheese Breath. What was a Cheese Breath?

Mona pondered all of these things in her dungeon room in between practice sessions for the night's talent show. She could barely focus on the poem she wanted to read aloud. Her brain was scrambled. Scrambled brains, she thought. Sounds like a perfect breakfast for zombies.

A knock at the door, and she spun to find Sal observing her. "Hi. It's very cold down here."

"Thank you," Mona said.

"Are you busy?"

Mona tossed the book of poetry onto the bed. "Just thinking about my talent. And Mama and Papa and zombies."

"Right." Sal wandered in and inspected some of her drawings, inky sketches of dresses and dark flowers and such. "These are good."

"A compliment. Thank you."

"You're not the only one who can find one good truth," he said quietly. "We have to set out tonight, you know. We have to go find Mama whether the spiders find the last twig or not."

"I agree."

"Are you nervous about your pageant thing?"

Mona shook her head. "No. Tonight is the talent night. I am quite prepared."

"Oh dear."

"I might not win."

Sal shrugged. "I can sneak you on the boat."

"I can sneak myself on the boat," she said, but in a joking way. They looked at each other and laughed.

"So." Sal shuffled back and forth, one foot to another. Like he wanted to say something but wasn't sure how to phrase it. "I don't know why I want to tell you this, but I do. I met a new friend. At the dump. That's why I go there so much. She said she would come to the carnival tonight, meet everybody."

"*She?*" Mona nearly spat the word. "Is this like a crush? What's wrong with you?! Sal!"

"She's a friend," Sal specified. "She's interesting. Really smart. You'll like her." He spun around suddenly, as if he were a little embarrassed to be talking about her at all. "She said she would see us tonight."

"Hey, Sal," Mona called out. He turned to look at her.

She hesitated. Mona wanted to warn him: be

careful who you trust. Especially right now. But she needed to find one good thing in her brother too. Maybe it's just as important to talk about the good things you see in your family. They're the easiest to take for granted.

"I'm excited to meet her," Mona finally said. Sal smiled and ran up the stairs.

Late that afternoon, the Problems finally left their house. They traveled quietly down Main Street, then onto the forest path. Desdemona O'Pinion could be anywhere waiting to strike. The pageant was tonight—that meant the woman had hours to lurk and plot and prank. Plus Cheese Breath—what was he? Where was he?

A ruffling in the trees above pulled the Problim glances toward the branches. The purple-tailed squirrel bounded overhead like a tiny sentinel.

"It was nice of Grandpa to send him to watch over us," Mona said. "He's a very realistic robot, isn't he?"

"I've thought about that," Thea said. "I think Grandpa loved him so much the squirrel felt like he was real. And if you decide you're real, who gets to tell you otherwise?"

"That's very deep," Mona said with a sigh.

*"Dark and deep,
deep and dark,
with or without
a beating heart."*

Frida ran ahead of all the Problims today, zigzagging so quickly along the path she barely made a sound.

Today, especially, Mona felt oddly comforted by the little squirrel. And the little fox. Strange how such funny little creatures made her feel more brave about what might lie ahead.

Mona stood backstage with the other contestants as Mayor Wordhouse gave the night's announcements. "I'm delighted to announce, after much deliberation, the judges have finally come to a consensus on the winner of the Pie Bake-Off. Wendell Problim! Come on up here and get your ticket to the Pirates' Caverns!"

The siblings cheered when he walked onto the stage. Mona let out a deep breath of relief . . . and anxiety. That just left her, Thea, and Frida.

"Is there anyone you'd like to thank, Wendell?" Mrs. Wong asked him as she gave him his sparkling corn dog trophy. At first, Mona didn't think her brother would speak at all. He stood in shock, rosy-cheeked with his glasses sideways. Like always.

Thea, who was backstage covering the pageant for Midge Lodestar, walked up beside Mona, sniffling. "I'm so proud of him! I don't even have real words to say. Just heart words."

Mona understood that. As much as she loved to test and try her siblings, she also liked it when they achieved cool things.

Wendell took the microphone from Mrs. Wong and cleared his throat. "I w-want to thank my m-mentors, the D-Donut sisters. Also m-my brothers and s-sisters. They gave me the id-dea for chocolate chip w-walnut pie."

"I want the recipe!" someone shouted.

Wendell chuckled nervously. "A-all right. Th-thank you."

Sundae snapped a pic for the scrapbook.

Thea dried her eyes again and pulled out a small handheld recording device:

Thea Problim here, reporting live from the final night of the Lost Cove Corn Dog Carnival for the Midge Lodestar show. Wendell Problim just became the youngest recipient of the

Bake-Off trophy! Best of all, he's earned his spot on the boat to see the Pirates' Caverns!

In other news, Farmer McCallister is still looking for his rogue piglets, who went missing after this week's coup d'toot. Toot Problim has been questioned. He responded in his own special stinky way, as always. Farmer McCallister was so grossed out he was unable to continue the conversation. If you see his piglets, Farmer McCallister asks that you please don't toot him about it. Just give him a call.

Tonight is also the big night when the new princess of the Lost Cove Corn Dog Carnival will be crowned. Carly-Rue O'Pinion has been the reigning princess for three years straight now. But this year has proven that anything can change. Settle in and enjoy our final festivities, friends. Remember, until we meet again, you are seen and loved.

"They should announce the winner of the creative writing contest soon," Mona said.

"Oh." Thea nodded. "They already did. The night of the spider incident." Thea blushed. "LeeLee and I tied for first place."

"Thea!" Mona exclaimed. She was truly thrilled for her sister. "Why didn't you tell anybody? That's great! That just leaves me and Frida! And I guess it means LeeLee is coming with us to the Pirates'

Caverns. Not a bad thing. She's smart."

"Oh, she said she didn't care about the caverns," Thea said. "She just wanted the free movie passes or something. I thought we could give her ticket to Frida. Frida's awfully good at sneaking around on her own though. Seriously, nobody ever sees her."

Mona had noticed the same thing, especially during the pageant. Frida was currently doing a handstand in the center of the backstage area and nobody even glanced her way.

"Fair enough." Mona shrugged. "I'll be glad when this"—she gestured to the flowery pageantry all around her—"is over. If I hear the word *pretty* one more time . . ."

Thea smiled sadly. "That's very easy to say when you've been called pretty your whole life. Don't get me wrong—I get that there are more important things like bravery and smarts and kindness and spider-training skills. But sometimes I wish people would call me pretty. Beautiful. Whatever." She shrugged. "I know it's silly but it's true."

"It's not silly," Mona said. "You're better than pretty, though. You get that, right? You're beautiful in ten thousand kinds of ways."

Thea smiled. "That's a very sisterly thing to say."

"Well, I kind of like being your sister. Don't let it go to your head."

"I'll try not to," Thea said with a laugh.

"I feel like I'm going to let everybody down if I don't win," Mona admitted. The truth had just flowed out of her, like word vomit.

"You've got this," Thea said. "Trust your gut, Mona Problim. We are so close. Frida's turn next. Then you. Good luck!"

Quickly, before Mona knew what was happening, Thea squished her close in a hug. Then she scampered back to the front row to continue reporting.

It was nearly Mona's turn. The big moment. Her moment.

The girl currently onstage was juggling oranges. I would have at least juggled something sinister and challenging, thought Mona.

"Hello, Mo,
I like your hair.
For my talent, I have
an impression to share."

Mona turned to see her sister standing there. Frida wasn't wearing a white dress. She was wearing the same fox-eared hoodie as always.

"You didn't dress up," Mona said to her. "Bravo!"

Frida beamed.

"I'm only good at being me,
It's all I've ever aspired to be."

The juggler left the stage and Mrs. Wong returned to the microphone. "And now, doing her impression of the great dreamer Ponce de Léon, we have Frida . . . Problim?"

Why did she keep saying her name like it was a question? Mona wondered.

Frida bobbed out onstage as if her feet were made of bouncy balls, spinning to the center. She took a bow and pulled a spyglass from the front of her overalls.

Mona paid special attention to the crowd as Frida performed. People were scrolling through their phones. Whispering to one another. But they always did that, didn't they? Nobody really paid attention to their lives anymore. They paid attention to a silly screen. The Problim children—minus Sal—sat in the front row, enraptured by the fox's performance. Was he with the friend he spoke of? Was he meeting her somewhere?

Frida cartwheeled to the front of the stage again and whispered softly,

"Dare to dream,
be bold and true,
and there's an adventure waiting for you too."

She stood to take a bow. The Problim children clapped and cheered. (When Alabama saw them applauding, he did too. But he didn't seem to know why.)

Frida ran backstage to Mona, beaming.

"I did my best.
It's up to you.
Show the world what Mona Problim can do."

Frida crooked her finger for Mona to lean over, so she could whisper a secret in her ear: "I'm so terribly-totally proud of you."

The fox scampered away, but her words lingered like blown-out birthday candles. *I'm terribly-totally proud of you.* That was a truth, a good one. It was a fine thing to hear. It was a fine thing to share with someone too.

Carly-Rue took her place behind Mona with a peculiar frown on her face.

"What's wrong?" Mona asked.

Carly-Rue shrugged. "My mom picked my talent for me. I'm singing, again. And I love to sing. I'm a country-pop singer, but . . . I had another idea. I had it prepared. Then I performed it for her last night and . . ." Carly shrugged. "She wasn't into it. She said it was fine, but not a winning talent. She said it's more of a boy's talent."

"Can I offer some advice?" Mona asked. Carly-Rue nodded.

"Your mom is not in this talent show. Do what you love."

"My parents said the same thing," said Melody Larson. Xena led her up to the girls, then sat quietly against her side. "I wanted to do a stand-up comedy routine and they said no, my brother's the funny one. They told me to play my piano—"

"That frustrates the daylights out of me!" LeeLee said. "I don't understand why people always think boys are leaders, better thinkers. I have a teacher who only calls on boys in class. For real, only boys. It drives me crazy because I know the answers too!"

"Everybody says my brother is so funny," Melody

Larson added. "And he is! But . . . I'm funny too. I feel like people see me one way, and that's it. But it's like you said in your answer the other night, Mona. I'm lots of things. Lots of ways."

"This is our talent show," Mona said. "Not anyone else's. So I suggest we stage a coup d'toot. If your talent tonight clearly expresses your heart and mind, I say go for it. If not, rethink it. Forget what boys are supposed to do or what girls are supposed to do. Just do what you love. Whatever makes your heart feel fiery."

"What makes your heart feel fiery?" Carly-Rue asked.

Wild adventures with her siblings. Starry nights in the swamp. The time she found a bone-stick in Grandpa Problim's house. She had been all alone, just her, but she'd done it! Running through the woods in the fall. Howling at that ever-present moon when it was full and wide and waiting for her to react. Life was dangerous and weird and full of people she loved. She was grateful for that.

"Lots of things," Mona admitted. "But tonight I want to read a poem I like."

"And I'm going to do *my* talent!" Carly-Rue said. "Coup d'toot!"

"Coup d'toot!" the girls said in unison.

Carly-Rue ran around the front of the stage, where Will was sitting with his mask over his eyes. (Will was tech support for the corn dog carnival. As far as Mona had seen, that meant plugging in the microphone every night.) "Come with me," Carly-Rue said to him, grabbing his arm and pulling him backstage. "I need your help with something. . . ."

"Next up, Mona Problim will recite a poem."

Mona strode out from backstage and took her spot in the center. Everyone quieted, waiting eagerly for what she might do.

She'd hoped her parents—both of them—would see her tonight in the talent show. She'd imagined it a thousand times. Imagined how special she would feel if they could all be together. Mama and Papa Problim had always encouraged Mona to be . . . well, Mona.

Maybe they'll be home tonight, she thought. Maybe they were a quick boat ride away.

I cast my desires into the sea, and the sea returns them back to me. If they're truly meant to be.

"Be there waiting for me," she whispered like a wish. Like a prayer. The deepest desire of her heart, cast into the sea.

She took a deep, centering breath. The rain was gone now; it had cooled the world considerably and beautifully. The clouds were rolling above, and Mona could see a patch of moonlight bleeding through.

There are different ways to howl, she decided. There are many ways to be heard. And her heart was fluttering tonight, eager as a bound-up bird to break loose. To do something exciting. To be seen, in a good way.

"Tonight," Mona began, "my talent will be reciting my favorite poem, 'The Raven,' by Edgar Allan Poe."

Several people nodded at her choice. More Poe fans, she realized. Maybe the Lost Covians had excellent taste! Sundae gave her a proud thumbs-up. It was Mama Problim who read Edgar Allan Poe to her years ago, when she wanted a bedtime story that was a bit darker. Mona had never cared for traditional fairy tales. Most of those were love stories—which was fine, if that's what someone's into—but she wanted adventure. Her mama understood.

As Mona recited the poem, she pretended to be in the story. She stomped her foot against the stage at the part where the Raven knocked on the door. And for her finale, at the end, she spread her arms open wide and the circus spiders swirled down around her, landing on her shoulders. They sent web strands shooting from her shoulders, connecting like mighty wings on her back.

Violet O'Pinion had been right. Wearing wings did make Mona feel different.

When Mona ran backstage, the other contestants swarmed her. And she didn't even mind. She smiled, genuinely, as they gushed about the talent they were ready to perform. Most of them had changed out of pageant dresses. They wore T-shirts, jeans, band uniforms, basketball outfits, costumes, and crazy hats. Mona had never seen the corn dog pageant before. But she had a feeling this was the best one by far.

"Where's Carly-Rue?" Mona asked. At the same time, Mrs. Wong announced the girl's name.

And Carly-Rue came from one of the backstage areas, where she'd been chatting with Will. She still wore her sparkly pageant dress, of course. But she'd also put on a pair of awesome, dark-rimmed glittery glasses. She winked at Mona as she passed her.

Mona gave her a thumbs-up. "Coup d'toot," she reminded her.

Carly-Rue O'Pinion walked out on the stage, and Mona peeked out to watch Desdemona's reaction. Carly-Rue walked past the microphone, and Desdemona's face sank into confusion. And then anger. Mona couldn't help but smirk.

Carly-Rue motioned for Will to help her set up a small table, her laptop, and a big canvas screen—so everyone could see what she was doing on the computer.

Desdemona waved her arms at her. "What are you doing?" she mouthed.

Thea leaned against Mona. "What is she doing?"

Mona shrugged. "Making her own rules."

Carly-Rue connected her laptop to the screen Will set up. And she began to explain basic computer coding, talking the audience through a new website she was developing to celebrate the lunch ladies at her school.

A good truth: underneath Carly-Rue's crown was a very cool mind.

When she passed Mona walking offstage, Carly-Rue was sparkling brighter than she ever had before. "I still like to shine," she said to Mona.

And Mona actually smiled, sincerely.

Thea Problim here, reporting on your final night of the corn dog carnival. Carly-Rue just earned a standing ovation for her computer coding wizardry. I don't know about you, but now I'm excited to get home and write a few programs too. Up next is LeeLee and . . . oh my, can you hear the music? It's thumping like a giant heartbeat from the stage! LeeLee is wearing her basketball jersey with her ballet tutu. I'm told this is a fusion, a dance combining two sports she dearly loves. Melody Larson is up next! She's doing a comedy routine, and the crowd is roaring. Even her service dog, Xena, looks like she's laughing at Melody's jokes! We'll know the winner soon, friends!

The rest of the contestants were all backstage, dancing, cheering each other on, when they heard the sound of a throat clearing. "Excuse me."

Mona was surprised to see Alabama Timberwhiff standing there. Well, she was sort of surprised. Alabama loved the pageant more than anybody. Maybe more than Desdemona and Carly-Rue. Seeing him there made sense. But his outfit was unexpected. Alabama wore a red satin suit and sequined tie. His hair had been sprayed into a perfect swoop on top of his head.

"Hey, all . . . ," he said, nervously. "I want to ask you something. I know this sounds . . . maybe strange. Or maybe not. I don't know how it sounds. I'm very nervous."

"You don't need to be nervous," Mona told him. "Cool suit, by the way."

"You really like it?" he asked. The sparkles reflected off his face. He wanted to shine too, Mona could see.

Mona nodded. "I think it's sensational."

"Good. You gave me some advice a few nights ago, and I'm taking it."

Mona felt a nervous twist in her stomach. She'd never been known for giving "good" advice. "Which is . . . ?"

"I'm making my own rules," he said softly. And then he laughed, nervously. He twisted his fingers together while he talked. "I have always, always, dreamed of being in the Lost Cove Corn Dog pageant. The rules say boys can't enter, but I can't stop thinking about it. And dreaming about it. I really want to do this. And this year, well, you've all kind of made it your pageant. So I thought maybe you could bend the rules, for me. I understand if you say no, but . . . can I be a contestant?"

The girls all glanced at each other, then back at Alabama.

"Of course," someone shouted.

"YES!" LeeLee hollered out.

"Wait." Carly-Rue pushed her way to the front of the crowd. Mona wondered if she would say no. Her mother had helped create this pageant. Technically, that probably did make Carly-Rue the boss of it all. Mona watched as Carly-Rue came to a stop directly in front of Alabama. Surely she wouldn't break his heart like this. Not when she'd just proven how cool she could be!

Carly-Rue put her hands on Alabama's satin shoulders. "I don't say yes," she told him, her voice low and serious. Some of the girls gasped. Mona was about to argue why this opinion was absurd. Then Carly-Rue's face broke into a wide grin. "I say, enthusiastically, ABSOLUTELY YASSSS!"

Alabama threw his arms around Carly-Rue's neck, and the rest of the girls hugged him.

The girls worked quickly to help Alabama get onstage. LeeLee slipped Mrs. Wong a note with Alabama's biography on it. She seemed confused, at first, reading over it. But then Alabama walked out onstage, his chin high, his sequined bow tie shining. He took center stage as the girls cheered.

Thea Problim here, reporting what is surely a first at the corn dog pageant. Alabama Timberwhiff has entered the pageant last minute and the girls, and the crowd, are cheering wildly. Mrs. Wong is reading his biography, saying this has been Alabama's dream since he watched his first pageant at three years old. Sometimes dreams take such a long time to come true . . . but that makes them even sweeter, doesn't it?

The crowd was silent at first. But then Alabama took the microphone and sang one of his favorite songs, a song from a Broadway play his parents had taken him to that summer. When the crowd stood and cheered, Alabama took a bow. And Mona could almost envision it: his heart's desire, caught on a sea breeze, floating back into his heart where it belonged.

And that's the end, friends! The judges are off to deliberate and decide who the corn dog princess will be . . . and who will win that final, coveted ticket to the Pirates' Caverns!

The judges deliberated for an hour. And Mona felt every single second. Patchy storm clouds peeled back now and then to reveal the moon, full and bright. Calling her onward to the caves. To her parents. To the treasure, maybe.

Time was ticking away to get to the Pirates' Caverns. What if Mama and Papa got there before the Problims did? What if they got stuck? They couldn't get the treasure. Only the seven could do that. Grandpa had told them so.

Mona tapped out a nervous rhythm on her skirt. Admittedly . . . she was also surprised by how much she wanted to win this thing. And also by how she'd enjoyed the last few moments.

"And now, if we could have all of our contestants come out onstage, we'll announce the winner of the Seventy-Seventh Annual Lost Cove Corn Dog Carnival Princess," Mrs. Wong said, opening an envelope. She smiled at the winner. "Our second runner-up is LeeLee Alapo!"

LeeLee's mom bounced out of her seat and squealed. And LeeLee bounced too—all the way to the microphone to get her certificate.

"Our first-place runner-up for Corn Dog Carnival Princess," Mrs. Wong said, opening another envelope, "is . . . Miss Mona Problim!"

Her heart sank. She could feel it, like an anchor

dropping from her chest down into her gut. That couldn't really happen, she supposed. She put on a fake smile for the crowd. She didn't want to seem like a jerk who was bitter about losing. But what would she do now? She had to be with her siblings. The seven had to be together. Sneaking Frida onto the boat wouldn't be hard. Frida was stealth. But sneaking Mona on . . . how would that actually work?

She couldn't even look at her siblings. Disappointment made her feel still, frozen. Finally it was Sal who caught her eye.

"I've got you," he mouthed. "It's okay."

It was a very big-brotherly thing to say. It was very kind.

Mona smiled, just a little bit more. But disappointment sat on her shoulders like a heavy old coat. Weirder still, somewhere along the way, she'd begun really wanting to win this thing. Mostly for the Pirates' Caverns, of course, but also for reasons she couldn't explain. And that was okay. Disappointment isn't a bad thing, she realized. It's okay to feel that.

"And finally," Mrs. Wong said, "this year's princess of the Lost Cove Corn Dog Carnival is . . . Miss Carly-Rue O'Pinion! Carly-Rue, your family is welcome on the stage to celebrate with you!"

Mona looked at Carly-Rue and applauded, sincerely. She deserved it.

But the crowd went silent. At the end of the aisle of folding chairs stood Stan O'Pinion. And he was holding the hand of the girl with wings.

One Princess to Another

Mona could barely breathe.

Violet was with the enemy! The Big Bad! She knew they shouldn't have trusted her!

This was the man who'd started a feud with their grandfather. Who'd run him out of town. Dorrie had told them once that this man was the villain they should be afraid of. Not Desdemona. And Violet—their friend, *Violet*—was holding his hand! It was one thing to believe there were two sides to every story. But this felt wrong.

Violet's father, who looked like he'd just arrived back in town from one of his trips, ran to meet her in the aisle. "What are you doing out?" he shouted.

Violet looked up at her grandfather. He smiled, kindly. Just how grandfathers are supposed to smile. She squeezed his hand and said, "I want to be part of the world. Even if there's a risk of getting hurt. That's why you made this mask, so I could have some freedom."

Mona jumped off the stage to stand with her siblings. Sundae had disappeared somewhere. But the rest of her siblings huddled in close together, watching, not sure what they should do. Should they leave? Should they confront him? Before they had an answer, Violet approached them.

"Don't say anything," she said, uncertainty wavering in her eyes. "Just go. My window is unlocked. Go in, and go look in his room in the basement. The twig-tree was always especially active when Grandpa played music." Her eyelashes fluttered, as if she was very unsure of what she would say. "The last bone-stick is in his office somewhere, I'm sure of it. And remember . . . I love him. A lot. Maybe there are two kinds of truth here. Maybe truth can hurt people just as much as lies do. Let's end this feud for them if they won't do it themselves."

Carly-Rue caught Mona's sleeve. The new crown sparkled extra bright beneath the carnival lights.

"I'll keep my mom occupied for as long as I can," she whispered, passing Mona a silver ticket.

Mona looked back and forth between them. "How much do you know?"

Carly-Rue shrugged. "As much as I need to. You're not the only one who likes to get to the bottom of things. Good luck in the caverns."

A quick smile, and Carly-Rue ran back up onstage to have pictures taken with her family. And Mona came to a somewhat sad conclusion: she no longer had a nemesis. It would be impossible to hate Carly-Rue now. She wasn't terrible. Not even a little bit. She was pretty darn cool. A fine opponent. A formidable foe.

"Hurry," Violet whispered, and she jumped onstage to join her family. The O'Pinions. Mona watched them pose for the camera, arms around each other, congratulating Carly-Rue. They looked so normal. A few of them—most of them?—were actually pretty great. The enemy was becoming so difficult to dislike.

"Let's go," Sal said, pulling Mona's sleeve. She shoved her silver ticket in her pocket and ran for the woods.

While Frida and Toot stood watch outside, Mona entered the O'Pinion house through Violet's room. (Mona should go first, they decided. She was the best at creeping.) Wendell, Thea, and Sal followed behind her. Thea fed Biscuit a donut, then Wendell swooped her up in his arms.

"That dog can't be trusted," Mona reminded him. Biscuit nipped at her.

"We need an ally," Wendell explained. Biscuit wiggled her tail at being chosen.

The house was eerily quiet when they opened Violet's door and descended from her tower room. Mona walked down the same hall she had on her first snoop. "I know they're all at the carnival," Sal said. "But I still feel like we should be extra sneaky."

The rest of the Problims agreed; they blended with the shadows down the hallway, down the stairs, and into the kitchen.

Thea sighed sadly. "This feels a lot like breaking and entering," she whispered. "I don't like the thought of being a common criminal."

Mona patted Thea's shoulder, causing her to jump. "There's nothing to worry about, Thea. You are anything but common."

"It's so dark," Sal observed.

"I can see fine," Mona reminded him. "Put your hand on my shoulder, Sal. Everybody hold on and let me lead."

"That's the scariest thing you've said all day," Sal mumbled.

Mona was delighted by the darkness. She thrived in it. She was much more comfortable using her night vision to snoop. She led her siblings through the finely furnished home—which reminded her of a much nicer, newer version of the Problim home—all the way to the top of the basement stairs. Soft light beamed from down below.

Sal pulled the water witch from his sleeve and passed it to Wendell. "Maybe if you hold it, the witch will lead you to the missing stick."

Wendell sighed. "Th-things are about to g-get w-wild, then."

"Not necessarily," Mona said. She pulled off her second-place sash and wrapped it around the end of the stick. "Unless all seven of us are connected, the world doesn't go wild. But wrap this around the end anyway. Maybe you won't have weird visions if it doesn't come in contact with your skin."

"That's not a horrible idea," Sal conceded.

Actually, it was a fantastic idea. Wendell wrapped

his fingers around the stick and . . . he wasn't shoved into a water trance. The ground didn't shake and the storms didn't kick up outside.

"Do you feel anything?" Thea asked her brother.

"Not yet," he said. "But—wait—whoa!" With a jerk, the stick tugged Wendell toward the stairs. His rear hit the top step and he bounced down the rest of the way, holding on to the edge of the stick as it pulled him toward the far corner of the room.

Whack!

The edge of the stick flopped down hard on the desk.

"Okay," Sal said. "The twig's in here. Let's search the desk."

"This feels so wrong," Thea told him.

"Technically, it is wrong," Mona mumbled. "That's what's so fun about it."

Mona's siblings snooped through the desk. But a picture on a bookshelf had caught her eye. The tall man, Stan, beside a smiling woman who must have been his wife. Two girls were in the picture too. One was clearly a younger Desdemona; even then the big sunglasses were in place. But the other face . . . that face looked most familiar. It was the same face she'd seen in the photograph upstairs.

Frida the Fox pounced beside Mona to look in the picture.

"What should we say?
What should we do?
This woman is a taller version of . . . you."

And then Thea was standing at Mona's other side. She let out the sweetest gasp and said, "Is that . . . Mama Problim?"

The Problims were rifling through the drawers, trying to find the final—final!—twig. But Mama Problim's name made them stop momentarily. She was the only thing better than buried treasure.

"What?" Sal snapped up from the desk.

"Look!" Mona put the picture down on the desk, for Sal to lean over and look. His eyes widened. And then Thea shouted, "EUREKA!"

Gently, Thea held up a violin resting in the chair in front of the desk. On the back of the violin, fitted into a carved-out hollow made specially for it, was another bone-stick. The last. "We've got it," Thea whispered.

Wendell took it. This time, without any hesitation, he popped the last piece into place. A soft, golden light filled the room around the twig. The light faded, but the glow in Wendell's eyes didn't.

Sal raised an eyebrow. "Nothing happened. I didn't feel like the earth was sucking me into it. The sky didn't open. What's the deal?"

"It's not the stick that makes the earth reveal its treasures," Mona said. "It's us. When we join hands, that's when the world goes wild."

"We d-did it," Wendell said. "And I can already f-feel it is pulling me back toward the carnival! Let's go! Let's go!"

"Wait." Mona held up the picture. "Look at this first. Who does this look like to you?"

"It looks like you, Mona," came a soft, vicious voice from the doorway. The children spun to see Desdemona standing there, watching them. "It looks like you because that's your mother . . . who also happens to be my sister."

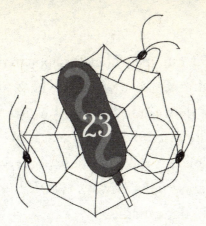

The Water Witch

That's impossible," Mona said to the dragon lady. But in her heart, she knew it wasn't impossible. Not at all. She was holding the proof in her hands.

Desdemona smiled. "Look at the picture again, Mona. You know it's her. All of you do. Mina O'Pinion was always jealous of me. She took everything I love. And she disgraced our family name when she ran away and married your father, Major Problem."

"You were friends with him too," Mona said. "He told me."

"More than friends," Desdemona said, her voice cracking. "She took him from me. She took everything from me. They disappeared for years. Your grandfather always knew where they were, of course. But he wouldn't tell us. I heard rumors they moved to the Swampy Woods years ago. But it's like a barrier covered those woods. Some wild, unruly weather catastrophe always swirled around that place. Dark, dark magic."

Mona wasn't even thinking of this anymore. She couldn't hide the grimace from her face. "So, you're my aunt?"

"Oh yes." Desdemona looked equally upset. "You're named after me, in fact. Lucky you."

This revelation was too much. "I'm going to vomit," Mona said, leaning back against the desk. A quick blue shimmer on the stairs caught her eye. She squinted at them, trying to get a better look, but the shimmer was already gone.

"Do what you must," Desdemona told them. "In the meantime, I will take the water witch."

"N-no!" Wendell pulled it behind his back.

"You can't take it," Thea told her.

"Watch me," Desdemona said, moving toward them.

The Problim children gathered around Wendell, standing in place.

"No," Mona said. "She means you really can't do it. Wendell is a water witcher. It only works for him."

Desdemona didn't look convinced. She moved toward them again.

Mona looked her aunt in the eye. "If you try to hurt him, you'll be sorry. We can level this house to the ground if we want. You know it's true."

Desdemona stopped cold at that. Mona had known Desdemona hated them from the start. But now something else was clear: she was afraid of them. She was afraid of the power they had when they were together.

"We're going to go now," Sal said. "And we're going to find this treasure, and make everything right again. It's time for this feud to be over."

"You won't get far," Desdemona assured them. "I'm not the only one out there looking for you."

"We know all about Cheddar Biscuits," Sal said.

"Cheese Breath," Thea whispered.

"Whatever." Sal shrugged. "When we're together, we can handle anything. Even you."

Another blue shimmer snagged Mona's attention, first from the stairs. Then from the corners of the room. Violet's circus spiders, who'd been scrambling into the room for some time, formed a cage around Desdemona.

Desdemona snarled. "You think spiders will cage me? Not all O'Pinions are afraid of them, you wicked little snots."

A loud, fluttering sound erupted upstairs. Mona only registered golden flecks at first—sparkling all around them—before she realized a cavern of wattabats was swirling around Desdemona O'Pinion. Was this Sundae's doing? Or the mechanical squirrel's? Wattabats weren't cooperative with just anybody.

"Outrageous!" Desdemona screamed. "You children are bewitched."

The bats wouldn't hold her for long. But it would get them time to get to the island, at least.

"This doesn't matter!" Desdemona screamed. "He will find you. And I will too, eventually. Your father is gone. You have no parent to watch over you. If you make it out of those caves alive—which I doubt—you better pack your bags, little Problems."

"We're already packed," Mona told her. Desdemona didn't move as the children ran around her to climb back up the stairs. Only Mona waited. Desdemona glared at her through her fluttering gold cage of bats and spiders.

"You knew we were your nieces and nephews all along?" Mona asked.

Desdemona smirked. "You could have been imposters."

"You knew we weren't, though," Mona said. "And you still tried to send us to seven different continents."

Desdemona said nothing. She only stared at Mona.

"You are cruel, Aunt Desdemona."

The Problims ran out of the house as a dark storm cloud swept over the moon.

"Do you see what this means?" Sal said as they raced back toward the carnival grounds. "We're Problims . . . and we're O'Pinions. We're both."

The knowledge felt awfully heavy to carry in their hearts. Mona was glad her siblings were with her. Glad she didn't have to carry it alone.

The Pirates' Caverns

The witch will help, but you must lead. . . .

The riddle rolled through Mona's mind as Wendell took the completed bone-stick, the water witch, off his back. "Okay. Let's see if this does what we think it does. Let's go find Mama."

Wendell held the water witch in front of him, like a fine knight holding a sword. My brother has never looked braver, Mona realized. "Do you feel anything?"

Wendell swallowed visibly, and took a long, deep breath. He lurched forward with so much force that he would have fallen forward, if Thea hadn't grabbed him. "Yes."

"Stay calm," Mona suggested. "Try to get used to it. Let it guide you."

Wendell clenched his jaw and stood very still. His eyes were closed.

"Do you see Mama Problim?" Mona asked. "Is she okay?"

Wendell was silent for a moment. Then he shook his head, slowly. "Just w-water. But I c-can control it." His arm tensed and stretched long. "I d-definitely feel it now!"

Wendell began moving, witch extended in front of him. Thea kept a hand on his shoulder. Mona and Sal had to hustle to keep up. (Mona hoisted Toot up on her shoulders.) A stripe of lightning forked the sky, just as the six stepped into the Bagshaw Forest.

The siblings paused for a second at the top of the hill. The carnival grounds looked very different at night. Especially the rides. Standing on the hill, the rides looked like skeletons, Mona thought. Looming skeletons waiting to come alive and attack. *Boooones.*

"Still all right, Wendell?"

He nodded, arm still straight. Knuckles white on the hand holding the witch.

"W-what if Ch-Cheese Breath is down there?" he asked.

"Don't be afraid," Mona said. "We can handle anything together."

"And I'm really not afraid of someone called Cheese Breath," Sal said.

"Then o-onward and up-pward," Wendell said. "T-to Narnia and the n-north!" He led them down the hillside. Then, turning a right at the carnival gate, they headed toward the beach. A small boat bobbed in the water, and Alex Wong and Sundae stood in front of it.

Toot squealed, and tooted,[25] and the rest of the Problims joined in with exclamations of their own. "We got it right!" Thea shouted. "We're going to the caverns!"

"There they are!" Sundae shouted. "And they've got it all together. GLORY!"

Alex Wong couldn't have cared less about whatever she was shouting about. He only stared at Sundae. Mona shook her head; Alex didn't even try to hide it. Cartoon hearts might as well be floating out of his eyeballs.

Mona cleared her throat. "Sundae . . . is he okay

---

25 **#44**: The Tooty Jubilee: A celebratory, joyous toot—always emitted in a series of three. Smells like the burp that happens after eating apple pie.

to be here?" She nodded to Alex.

Sundae patted Mona's shoulder. "Alex is a trust-worthy friend. The animals agree." Happy Henry tumble-flew out of Sundae's sling and landed on Alex's shoulder like a pirate's parrot. Sundae giggled.

Sal pulled a flashlight from his belt and shone it in his older sister's face, making her flinch. "Where have you been? We looked all over for you when we left the pageant to get the last twig. We had to face Desdemona—we nearly got separated—and you weren't there!"

"I'm so sorry." Sundae looked at Alex. Her cheeks flushed red. "We were taking a walk on the beach. I lost track of time. The moon tonight was GLO—"

"Focus," Mona said, cutting Sundae off before she could add any frilly details. She grabbed Sal's flashlight and shone it over the boat. Not that she needed a light. Mona had perfect night vision. She did this for the benefit of her siblings. "We need to get to the Pirates' Caverns now before the tide gets too high."

She could feel the tide rising; it was an emotion as strong as joy or fear or pure delight. There was a vibration between the moon and the tide, a dance Mona somehow felt part of in a way she never had before. Time was short. They had to move quickly.

Alex jumped into the boat, stretching out his hand to help the siblings inside and giving them each a fitted life jacket. "If I'd known you were trying to get there, I could have taken you over anytime."

"Thanks for telling us that now," Mona mumbled. She didn't think Alex would hear her. But he did, and he chuckled.

"Sorry. It's your fault, you know. Sometimes it's okay to ask for help. Even if you're a Problim."

"That's debatable," Mona replied.

Toot puffed a rancid #11.[26]

Alex teetered, and Sundae leaned into his side, pulling a clothespin from her pocket. "Here you go. His toots take some getting used to."

Alex blinked at her. "You're so thoughtful, Sundae. And so innovative."

"FOCUS!" Sundae's six siblings all screamed at once.

"GLORY!" Sundae shouted, clapping her hands. "What a night! Let's go to the caverns."

"Why do you say that?" Alex asked, pushing the

---

26 **#11:** The Run-Amok: A silent but violent declaration that means: let's have some fun! Smells like week-old sushi.

boat from the shore and revving the engine. "What's the glory story?"

"Maybe you can just tell it quietly to each other," Mona suggested. The rest of the Problms nodded eagerly. But Sundae didn't seem to hear them.

Mona looked toward the island—the caverns— and wished she could propel the boat forward by her will alone. They were so close to Mama now!

"Have you heard of Flannery O'Connor?" Sundae shouted over the sound of the roaring sea. Water sputtered against the side of the boat as Alex glided it away from the shore. "She was a classic Southern writer, a brilliant woman. She raised peacocks in her yard. There's a story about her that says one day, a lady walking past saw the peacock unfurl its royal feathers. And the lady stopped walking, dropped everything in her arms, and shouted, 'GLORY.' She was overwhelmed by the unexpected beauty. I love that idea; the thought that glory is waiting around the corner to take your breath away. I think it's a sweet way to live. Life's a peacock, know what I mean?"

Alex shook his head. "You're amazing, Ice Cream Sundae."

Sundae beamed at him. "You're a peacock, Alex the Great."

"Please," Mona begged. "Stop. I cannot take anymore. This is a very serious task ahead. We need to prepare mentally."

Alex steered the boat around the perimeter of the carnival, which looked quite different from this vantage point. Dull safety lamps had been left on in each of the small kiosks. Mona saw a stand full of dolls and teddy bears with strange black button eyes hanging by threads. The Ferris wheel cast a large spidery shadow over the grounds. The seats made a low, creaking sound as they rocked in the breeze.

Sal nodded as the boat passed by. "At night, this looks like a place where creepy clowns have meetings."

Mona agreed. "It's beautiful, isn't it? Makes me want to redecorate my room."

"Next stop, Pirates' Caverns!" Alex said.

Then the boat curved away from the shore and slicked a line across the angry sea. The Problims all grabbed on to the edges of the boat as the waves jostled them back and forth. They'd never been out in the ocean before.

Mona found herself leaning into Sal, who was leaning into Thea. Her siblings were like magnets, she realized, they were always leaning toward each other—longing to click—just like the pieces of the water witch. Together, they would save their parents from whatever predicament they were in.

"I'm glad we're all doing this together." It was a good truth: there is no one better to have an adventure with than a sister. Than a brother.

"Mona," Sal said. She braced herself for some snide remark. "Sometimes you're tolerable."

"Up ahead," Alex called over the roar of the sea. "You can see them. The Pirates' Caverns! Many pirates hid out in those caves back in the day, supposedly." Alex turned back and winked at Sundae. "And there are all sorts of rumors about ghosts and treasures down in the depths. Really, it's the bioluminescence that people mistake for magic. We'll go down into one of the caves, if you'd like, so you can see what it looks like. Shiny freckles on the water."

Sundae sighed.

The rest of the children shook their heads.

The caves sat on their own little island, barely a dot on the map. The Problems jumped from the boat onto the sand, looking back at the carnival with its creaky Ferris wheel and, past that, the foggy woods surrounding Lost Cove. It all seemed so small from here. Home was barely a dot on the horizon.

Alex passed out slick yellow parkas. "Rain's definitely on the way," he assured them, even as Sundae told him how smart he was. "Now—which cave would you like to explore?"

The Problim children looked all around. Then they looked at Mona with a question in their eyes. A big question.

Where was Mama Problim?

This scene was exactly like Mona's vision. The clouds peeled back to reveal the full moon—her moon—shining down on this moment she'd anticipated for so long. But there was no Mama. Were they too late? Had they misunderstood the whole thing?

Mona looked at Wendell. "Do you feel any tension in the witch?"

Wendell held the witch out in front of him, closing his eyes. He waited, still and silent.

Alex Wong cleared his throat. "What . . . are we doing exactly?"

"Shhhh," Sundae said. "Just follow along."

The water witch jerked Wendell toward the left. His eyes snapped open. "Yes! I feel it. It's pulling into that cave—the really creepy entrance over there that looks like a skull mouth!"

"Perfect," Mona cooed. "We pick *that* cave, Alex. Wendell will lead the way."

"Something wonderful is about to happen," Sundae said. Alex followed behind her, his hand on her shoulder.

"Or something terrible," Thea whispered, popping the hood of her parka.

Either way, Mona thought, this night will bring something dangerous. And Mama Problim might already be there—somewhere in the thick of it all—waiting for their help.

A Formidable Foe

Be back soon, Tootykins," Sundae said, kissing her baby brother's soft head. Toot Problim puffed a toot of solidarity.[27]

Mona nodded. "That's wise of you," she told him.

Toot had decided to guard the cave.

"You'll alert us if you see anything suspicious," Sundae told him. "Anything!"

Toot nodded, and cuddled close to Ichabod.

Mona was so proud of Toot. "Together we might

---

27 #211: The Motto Fart: A flatulent trumpet of Toot's life philosophy: fart loudly and proudly and be brave and courageous.

rule the world someday," she told him. He tooted a #173[28] in response, the Appreciation Flatulation.

"Mona should walk behind Wendell," Thea said. "Since she can see so well in the dark."

Wendell gulped. "That's even scarier than being in a d-dark c-cave!"

"I won't do anything," Mona said, clapping a hand down on his shoulder. "Truce tonight. No pranks."

Wendell nodded (though he didn't believe her totally) and led his siblings into the cave. He kept the water witch extended in front of him like a sword.

"C-could someone shine a flashlight?" Wendell asked. "I kn-know Mona can s-see but I d-don't want to trip."

"No," Mona whispered sharply. "Trust me. If someone sees our light they'll follow. Just lift your feet when you walk."

"How else do you walk?" Sal asked.

Mona rolled her eyes. "Can you feel the water witch leading you, Wendell?"

~~~~~~~~~~~~~

28 #173: The Appreciation Flatulation: A soft, graceful puff of wind that means: thank you. Smells like toe jam and strawberry jam mixed together.

"Y-yes! It feels like a giant m-magnet!"

"Good. Keep moving. I'm right behind you. I won't let you fall in a hole. Not today, anyway."

Mona kept her hand against the cave wall, so she'd stay balanced. It was chilly and wet and occasionally her fingers brushed past strands of plants that felt a little bit like human hair. She smirked as Alex Wong—in the far back behind Sundae—felt the same thing and let out an "UGH." The sound echoed all around them.

"Shh," Sundae reminded him, with a giggle. "We have to be quiet!"

Alex sighed. "My brother was right. Your family has an interesting concept of the word FUN. I can't see anything. . . ."

"It's okay," Sundae said, her voice sickeningly sweet. "Just hold on to me."

Gross. Mona sighed. Sal made kissy sounds in the dark until Thea punched him in the shoulder. "Pay attention, everybody! Follow Wendell and Mona or we'll get separated! This place is like a dungeon," Thea observed. "It reminds me a little of Mona's bedroom."

"I hope my walls are this damp and mossy someday," Mona said.

"Yes?" Sundae called from the back. "Did you need me, Mona?"

"I said someday, not Sundae."

"Oh. Well. While I have your attention," Sundae said, "I wanted to say your answer during the pageant Q&A was . . . lovely. And so was your talent. And you seemed to really bond with those girls. Even Carly-Rue O'Pinion, who I was sure was your worst enemy."

Mona sighed. "She's not that bad. I'll have to find a new enemy, I guess."

"I'll always be your foe," Sal said. "And your friend." Mona nodded. This was true of brothers the world over, she assumed. Really, Desdemona was in the running for Worst Enemy #1. The spiders and wattabats couldn't keep her locked up forever. She'd surely try to get the Problems thrown out of town soon.

And what about Stanley O'Pinion? Was he a friend or foe? He'd looked like a kind old man when he walked into the pageant with Violet.

Violet. Violet trusted him. She loved him, Mona could see it. And Violet was a very smart girl.

"It's pulling so hard now!" Wendell shouted. "It's right ahead! V-very close!"

Sundae scrambled to the front and turned on her lantern, shedding light all around the area they were in. It looked like a room, almost; an opening in the cave with high ceilings. The darkness had made them feel like they were in a tunnel, but there was plenty of space up and around them. Ahead of them was a dead end, what looked like an avalanche of rocks.

Mona's heart sank. "She's not here. Why isn't she here?"

"Maybe she's on her way?" Thea asked.

"D-do you s-see this?" Wendell leaned back, pulling against the magnetic hold of the water witch. "It's trying to pull me forward."

"So, let it," Mona said. "Trust it! Grandpa said it was fine! He said the witch will help, but you must lead."

The twigs pulled Wendell to the rocky avalanche. And then slapped down hard on one large, flat rock in the center of all the rubble.

"Mama was here," Mona said. "There's something on this rock!"

There was no writing on the rock, like in her dreams. But a metal box was nestled into a hole that had been carved into the center of it. And inside the box was a letter in the familiar, scripted handwriting of Frank Problim.

"Grandpa's words!" Thea said again.

Mona read the clue aloud:

> WHAT ONCE WAS HERE
> IS MOSTLY CLOSED
> (SOME THINGS SHOULD NOT BE OPENED).
> BUT I FILLED MY JARS,
> ONLY TO LEARN
> THAT TIME CANNOT BE STOLEN.
> NOW, TAKE THE WITCH!
> SET SAIL! BE QUICK!
> WHERE THE STARS FALL INTO THE SEA,
> A FINAL DOORWAY OPENS WIDE,
> AND THERE A TREASURE TRUE WILL BE.

"You were right, Wendell," Mona said. "There's another fountain somewhere. Where the stars fall to the sea. . . ."

"B-but the w-witch is sticking h-here," Wendell

said. "It f-found something."

"Maybe because it avalanched over the first fountain?" Sundae asked. "Maybe it's sensing the water buried down beneath somewhere."

"Or maybe something else. . . ." Mona's mind was trying to recall something. Some piece of one of her visions. There was something she was forgetting. . . .

"Do you think she's already in the new place?" Sal asked, scanning the new clue. "Where the stars fall into the sea?"

"I think there's something here," Mona said, scanning the room. She focused her senses.

Ears alert to every sound.

Eyes focused in the darkness.

I am a wolf too, she thought.

Thea cleared her throat softly. She tucked the new clue into her parka. "At least we found that clue before Cheese Breath."

"That's not entirely true," came a low, crackly voice from the tunnel. Sundae shone the flashlight at the door just as two intruders stepped inside the cave.

One of them was an old man with a hat pulled low over his face. The other was a young girl, dark hair falling around her shoulders. In the girl's arms was Toot Problim. He saw his siblings and let out a lingering #4.[29]

"Ari?" Sal was confused. "Why are you holding Toot?"

"You know them?" Mona asked her brother, not taking her eyes from the shadows where the two new visitors lingered.

"I know her," Sal said. "She's the friend I told you about—"

"She's no friend of yours," the old man rasped, stepping out of the dark. His hands were bent like claws. And his shadow humped up behind him on the cave wall. Buzzard feathers, Mona thought. That's what his shadow reminded her of: hunched crows on the branches of trees in the swamp. This was one old bird.

"I don't care who you are," Mona said, teeth clenched. She wanted to bare them, like fangs. She'd never felt more wolfish than now. "Give me my brother."

"She's got her grandpa's fighting spirit," the old

---

29 **#4**: The Stink of Dread: A fart born of anxiety, foretelling a terrible event. Smells faintly of rotten eggs and vomit.

man said. Mona readied to pounce and the man said "No" with such a sharp finality that Mona stopped in her tracks. The room felt very cold all of a sudden. She could hear everyone breathing.

Mona had never been afraid of anyone until now. She did not like this feeling.

"Stay where you are, darling," the man said. "I'm capable of terrible things."

"But *you* aren't," Sal said to the girl, Ari, his voice pleading. The girl wouldn't look up. Toot kept his arms around her, as if he was comforting her. That was so like him, Mona thought. Comforting his captors!

"Tell us what you want," Sundae said. Alex kept trying to circle in front of her, but she shoved him out of the way. Alex didn't know her sister, Mona realized. He thought she was a girl in need of protecting. "As you can see, there's no fountain. It was destroyed years ago."

The man chuckled, pulling off his sunglasses to reveal a pair of pale blue eyes. "Oh, I know. I was here when it happened."

Mona couldn't tell if he was young or old. He moved slow, like a man who'd lived long enough to have lots of injuries, lots of pain. His face was smooth of wrinkles. But his face also reminded her of candle wax, slowly melting. He wasn't handsome or unattractive. He wasn't beautiful or plain. He looked almost like Mona imagined a ghost would look.

"Cheese Breath," Mona said. "I get it now."

The man grinned, his waxy face creasing. "Dear old Grandpappy Problim and his siblings tried to keep me away. But the weather was a giveaway . . . sure proof that another seven were now in the treasure-hunting business. And I kept contact with some folks in the area. I thought maybe Frank and his siblings had found another fountain. Now I know I was right."

"How could you have been here that long ago?" Mona asked. "And why are you two still holding Toot?!"

"You'll have plenty of time to think up questions before we see each other again. As for little baby Problim, he's coming with me."

Cheese Breath tickled the baby's chin. Toot bit him, hard. And farted.[30]

---

30 **#47: The Defensive-Offensive:** A toot used by Toot that creates an invisible, yet rancid, cloud of protection around those he loves.

Sal's nostrils flared with anger. "You aren't taking him anywhere. Ari, what are you doing?"

The girl wouldn't look him in the eye. "I promised I would help. I need the fountain too. My family needs it."

"It's not what you think," Sal said to her.

She made eye contact with him now. "How do you know? Have you actually seen it? Here's proof of what it does." She gestured to Cheese Breath. "He is . . . not a young man."

"How observant you are," Mona said, narrowing her eyes at the girl.

"Life eternal," Cheese Breath rasped. "If you keep drinking it. And my jar's run out, you see."

"Life eternal," Mona reiterated. "It doesn't look that way. You've got smooth skin but you're still a bag of bones. You're stuck at this same age forever. It's probably made you angry and violent—it did that to people."

"I'm going to explain the situation," Ari said softly. "We're taking Toot with us. I promise I'll keep him safe. Him and . . . the rest of your family."

Mona felt like she'd been punched in the stomach. Cheese Breath smiled as she—and the rest of her siblings—realized what she was saying.

"That's right." Cheese Breath nodded. "Mama and Papa Problim are spending some time with me, on my ship. Meet us at the island and take me to the fountain, and nothing bad will happen to them."

"You've got them." Mona barely breathed the words. She didn't know if she said them loud enough to register, until Cheese Breath turned his wicked smile on her.

"Indeed, I do."

"Ari!" Sal shouted. "Stop this."

Ari met Sal's stare, finally. "I'll take care of him. I promise. Your grandpa is leading you to the second fountain somehow. When you get there, you give us access to the water and Toot goes home with you."

"Just tell us where it is," Sal said. "And we'll all go together."

"Can't have you coming along," Cheese Breath said. "All seven of you would capsize my boat in no time."

Mona saw Ari counting quietly—six—and started over—six. Mona glanced around and saw no fox. Where was the fox? What was she doing? Was she hiding somewhere with Ichabod?

"We'll give him to you when we meet again," Ari said. "He won't be hurt. This can be very easy."

"It's not, actually," Mona said. "He's a toddler. He needs to eat regularly, or he gets really mad. You don't want to smell that toot."

Ari nodded. "I'll take care of him."

Cheese Breath smiled. "The quicker you meet us at the island and lead me to the fountain, the quicker we'll trade treasures. Take me to the fountain, and I'll reunite you with your family. And in the meantime, Toot will get to see his mommy."

Mona heard Thea sniffle and watched as a big tear dribbled down her face. "We didn't save her," Thea said.

Wendell curved his arm around his twin. "M-Mama is b-brave. She's okay, Th-Thea!"

"If you've hurt our parents," Sal said, his nostrils flaring, "you'll see what we're capable of."

"Oh, I have seen," Cheese Breath said. "And I fully intend to use it to my advantage. I have one more . . . errand to run before I can meet you at the island. Little Toot will come with me. For collateral. I trust that you can find your own way."

"You're not taking us with you?" Mona asked.

"Even though you need us to show you where the fountain is?" This villain's faulty logic gave Mona hope. Maybe he was a total idiot. Maybe taking back their parents and brother would be easy!

"Oh, you'll show me when you get there." Cheese Breath assured her. "I wouldn't want to ruin your grandpa's silly puzzles." The man smiled at her, but not kindly. "I must admit, the thought of all of you worried, and frightened, all alone on the sea . . . it delights me. We'll take this . . ."

He snatched Sundae's lantern from the rocks. And he and Ari began to back out through the opening.

Mona thought Toot would be crying, screaming in fear, tooting #1's[31] endlessly. But that's not what he did at all. Toot's eyes were narrowed. His tiny hands were balled into fists. He looked at his siblings, smiled, and farted a proud #45,[32] the Braveheart Fart.

He wants to help, Mona realized.

~~~~~~~~~~~~~~~~

31 #1: The I-Want-My-Mommy Fart: Smells like spoiled milk and mashed bananas. Toot's most desperate plea in times of deepest distress.

32 #45: The Braveheart Fart: The toot used by Toot to summon his courage and drive fear into his enemies' hearts. Smells like moldy cheese and sweaty victory.

Tootykins the Brave had ideas.

"Give us at least fifteen minutes before you come out of these caves. We'll see you soon, children," Cheese Breath said, "where the stars fall into the sea."

The Gift in the Nook

The Problim children waited—as they promised—fifteen minutes. Toot was too precious to risk.

"We should go," Sal said. "We don't owe any promises to him. Or her."

Sal was so embarrassed. Mona could hear it in his voice. And he should be, she thought. She almost pointed that out to him. But only because she was angry, and worried about her baby brother. Really, she could see how easy it would be to put your trust in someone only to have them break your heart somehow. That seemed to be a family legacy.

Sundae stared at her watch intently, and when it

read exactly fifteen minutes post–Cheese Breath, she charged ahead. "Lead, Mona. Go."

Alex Wong stood perfectly still, eyes unblinking, as if he was frozen in fear.

"Come on, you," Sundae said, looping her arm through his. "We have to move."

"Wait." Mona ran over to the rock.

"I have the clue," Sundae said. "Let's go." This was the most serious she'd ever sounded.

"Mama hid something in the nook of this rock," Mona told them. "I saw it in my night visions. And the water witch, it led us here even though the fountain was buried long ago. Someone give me a boost?"

Wendell lifted Mona so she could reach around deep in the nook. She saw nothing, but senses could be tricksters. So she closed her eyes and reached, hand scraping over gravelly dust and dirt.

"There's nothing!" Sal said. "Let's go!"

"Wait!" *There!* Her fingers traced over a small bundle—a capped vial, with a string around it. Inside the vial was the tiniest drop of water.

"Is that some of the water?" Sal whispered. "Should we go tell them? Maybe that's enough to get Toot back!"

"He wants the fountain," Mona said. "This led us down here, though. This is so we know we're on the right track, maybe."

And maybe this would come in handy later. What could you trade for a drop of magic water? Or who might you heal . . . ?

"See if there's anything else," Sal told her.

Wendell hoisted his sister up again, and she reached deeper into the nook. Past the dirt, Mona felt a mossy tangle. It felt good in a creepy, earthy way. Good like slimy walls and earthworms wiggling.

"I feel something," Mona said with a grunt. "But I just . . . can't . . . reach!" She wished she'd brought some of Sal's Wrangling Ivy. A clothes hanger. A back scratcher. Something! And then . . . Mona felt a small wriggle in the pocket of her cardigan.

A circus spider crawled out and scrambled across Mona's arm, then over her outstretched pointer finger. The spider disappeared into the moss. Not a second later—with tremendous effort—the spider dragged out the tiny something and pulled it into Mona's hand.

"Another zip drive!" Mona said. She gently petted the spider's tiny head. "Thank you." She slid the drive—and the spider—into her pocket, then raced around in front of her siblings to lead them out of the caverns and caves. The Problim children emerged onto the island to see a sky crackled by light. Morning was coming. But Tootykins, Cheese Breath, and that terrible girl, Ari, were nowhere to be seen.

"What about Frida?" Sundae asked. "Where did she go?"

"Problims, pile up!
The fox has arrived!
The fearless young Toot is fine and alive!"

Frida and Ichabod came running around the corner. Riding on Ichabod's back was the purple-tailed squirrel.

Alex Wong smashed his hands against his eyes. Then looked. Then hid his eyes again. "I don't understand anything."

"What did you see, Frida?" Mona asked.

"Brave Baby Toot
on a very large boat.

With a fart of the four winds,[33]
they set out to float!"

"And what about you?" Mona said, her voice thick with emotion. She tried to make eye contact with the purple-tailed squirrel. "Did you see anything that might help us? Do you know where this island is?"

The squirrel chattered something incomprehensible, and puffed out his chest. Mona slid the zip drive into the place where his heart should be. The squirrel bounced around in front of one of the large cave rocks and began projecting a video off the pale rocks. The countdown began, same as last time.

7 . . . 6 . . . 5 . . . 4 . . .

The Problim children moved closer to the image, waiting.

"What is this?" Alex asked Sundae.

"It's how Grandpa Problim left us messages," Sundae told him. "You'll see."

A kind old face suddenly filled the frame of the film.

---

33 **#35:** The Fart of the Four Winds: The flatulent rally of true adventure. Contains bold notes of fish in the ocean and chicken litter in a wide-open field.

"Hello there, my bold adventurers. My daring dreamers. Wherever I am right now, I hope you know that I am so proud of you. If you've found this film, you've made it as far as the old fountain. You've put the witch together, just as I asked. And I hope—soon—you'll be on your way to destroy the last fountain. Perhaps you know the story now.

"Years ago, as a boy, my siblings and I gave Cheese Breath—that terrible old rat—a jar of water from what we believed to be the fountain of youth so that he would leave and never trouble us again. Because in the process we realized something about that fountain—which was actually more of a stagnant creek. Yes, it was magical. But strangely, no animals would touch the thing. Plants that grew around the sides of it were gnarled, twisting around one another, choking the life out of each other. It might make things live longer. But it doesn't necessarily make them live well. Cheese Breath is human proof. His insanity knew no bounds. He vowed to hurt our families if we didn't give him the rest of it. Of course, by then, I only had two jars left that I'd hidden. So my six siblings and I waited until he sailed down the river. And then we made the river disappear, rolling like a wave back into the sea. After that, we surrounded this island—and the Swampy Woods—in a fog that was thick and wild. Magic, people called it. We really just made shapes in the fog—dragons roaring, open-mouthed lions, sharks leaping. It was enough to scare anyone away from here who didn't belong."

The siblings all looked at Sal, who'd created shapes in the fog many times. He nodded. "Smart."

"But what I knew," Grandpa continued, with sadness in his voice, "is that the water witch still had some give inside it. There was another fountain. By the time I was old, I knew the water in the jars couldn't be preserved. I did use it to clean the animatronics in my house once." He smiled. "Including a sweet old squirrel."

The squirrel flicked its tail.

"It has no ill effect on a robot, it seems. But the effect on people is severe and swift. Yes, it will make you last longer. But it takes away no pain, no illness. If anything, it fills your veins with venom. I hoped I could help Stanley O'Pinion see this, but . . . he was a grieving man. He was losing someone he loved. And faced with that proposition, living forever—in any state—is the decision most of us would make. I might have given it to him, because I loved them both so much. But his wife told me, adamantly, no. On the end of this film, you'll see a map . . . a map that will give you a quick route to the place where the stars fall into the sea. The place where, I believe, the final fountain of youth will be. Destroy it, children. For my sake. And for yours."

"The moral of this story," Sal said, "is that if a strange old man who smells like gnarly cheese and body odor asks for a twig from your magic tree, tell him noooo."

Mona nodded. "That's also what I gathered."

"I believe in you," Grandpa said. "I believe you are capable of true and wondrous magic. I believe—"

The film flickered suddenly, with little dots speckled all around. And now a new face filled the screen. A face shaped like theirs, with eyes they knew by heart and a voice made for lullabies. Mama Problim smiled at them.

Mona reached for her. She didn't even realize it was happening until her hand was in the air, as if her mama could actually reach back.

"If you are watching this," Mama said, "I want you to know that I'm trying to destroy this fountain so you don't have to. You don't have to go any further, children. Let me take care of this. Let me take care of you. I love you and adore you. I promise I'll be home soon."

A sound somewhere off camera caught Mama Problim's ear. The film flickered, then went out. And then, as promised, a map flashed up against the rocks.

Sal ran to the rocks and pointed. "These are the barrier islands around Lost Cove," he said. His finger traced up to the edge, to a set of islands that looked like the Big Dipper. "One of those, I guess?"

"The w-water w-witch will get us there if w-we get close enough," Wendell reminded them.

And then a sad silence stretched out between them. They were missing too many people. They had a thousand questions in their hearts. But only the sea replied.

Lost at Sea

The Problim children sat side by side on the beach, watching the sun continue its climb over Lost Cove. The boat ride back to Lost Cove's shore had felt long and quiet. That quiet still lingered all around them. The light glistened off the tears smearing their faces. This was the first time Mona had witnessed her siblings distraught at the sign of a problem. Granted, this problem involved her kidnapped baby brother and their missing parents. But still!

Wendell, Thea, and Frida were all huddled together, quietly sniffling into one another's sleeves.

"I knew something terrible would happen," Thea said with a sniffle, while she twisted her corn dog carnival T-shirt into knots. "I just didn't think it would be this bad!"

Sal sat staring at the sunrise, as if he could make it go backward, set again, start the bad week over. The sun stared back at him, pointing out all the angry (or was it sad?) lines on his face. Ichabod sat in Sal's lap, head resting against his shoulder. Even Sundae had nothing to say. She just lifted her face to the sunshine, held Happy Henry close, and kept her eyes closed. Alex sat beside her, arm around her shoulders.

"I don't know what we're waiting on," Mona said, jumping up off the beach. "Let's go."

"This is the biggest problem we've ever faced," Sal told her. "We need to think it through, don't you think? Not just react. We don't know where this island is, exactly, or what it's going to be like."

"We'll brainstorm as we go," Mona said. "This time we have to plan as we go, and we will. We'll get him back, Sal. We can't just sit around thinking about what to do. We have to start moving, and do things. Figure it out as we go. Come on!"

"Mona," Sal said bluntly. "They kidnapped our brother and our parents. If you're not just a little bit worried about that, maybe your heart really is made of ice."

"Sal," Sundae said. She tried to say his name as a warning—that he'd gone too far—but her voice was hollow today. Hollow because that's how she showed worry. But people don't always show how they're feeling in the same way.

"I don't worry the same way you do," Mona said. "I need to keep moving when I'm worried or anxious or afraid. Right now, though? I'm feeling a little confident. Because Cheese Breath stole Toot. How stupid was that? Toot will fart a force field of protection around himself and be perfectly safe. Of all the Problems to kidnap, he was the least-best pick."

Thea and Wendell's sad frowns twitched into a smile at this. Mona noticed. Even Sundae looked up, looked *hopeful.*

"We're smart and capable," Mona said, pacing back and forth across the hill. "That's what Cheese Breath doesn't realize. He can't outsmart us when we're all working together. We'll get Toot. We'll find Mama and Papa. We'll smash the treasure. We'll bury that island under the sea, if we have to. Grandpa knew we could do it."

"Toot's just so . . . so little," Sundae said with a sniffle.

"Yes, he's little," Mona conceded. "He's also a Problim. Toot is perfectly capable of handling himself. He's extraordinary. We all are."

Shock mingled with the sorrow in her siblings' eyes as they looked up at her. Why did people act like it was such a big deal when she gave a compliment? Because really, where her siblings were concerned, she could give zillions.

Mona rolled her eyes. "I tell you all the time," she said. "In my own way." She felt very deeply, in her own way. She'd work on doing a better job of showing them. People understand love differently. "Right now, I feel angry that some ancient idiot and his granddaughter kidnapped my brother. So, I'm doing something."

Mona dusted off her dress. "One step, then the next. That's how you avoid booby traps. Follow me!"

She didn't think they would. And she couldn't blame them. In the past, Mona had led them into various dark holes, tunnels, basements—all on purpose, of course. There would be time for that kind of fun in the future. First, she had to get Toot. She liked the little fellow. He was funny, he stank, he didn't talk too much (he didn't talk at all, really), and he fit perfectly in the human cannon she was forever modifying in the backyard.

The tall grass waved in the wind, backlit by the sun, as they moved down the hill. Mona heard someone behind her. She turned to see who it was, and the wind flung her black hair into her eyes.

Thea. Wendell. Frida.

Frida had her fox hoodie zipped up, ears extra pointy.

Sundae gathered up her pack and scrambled down the hillside next.

Sal stood still, staring at his siblings. Was he contemplating leaving?

"We have to do this together," Mona said. "That's in the riddle." And it was in their hearts, even before then. All siblings are capable of magic if they stick together.

Sal sighed and trudged down the path, tools jangling on his sleeves.

The ocean roared gently, bubbling foamy white against the rocks. The Problems walked along the shore to the place where the waves curled around the statue of Olivia the Great and Terrible.

Then a disgusting—and familiar—odor floated toward them on the wind. Mona paused.

Frida gasped. She jumped up on Wendell's shoulders and took a deep breath, wafting the air toward her face.

"Hold on to your dentures.
I smell adventure!"

"That's not adventure," Sal said, his nose wrinkling. "That's . . ."

"Toot!" Mona shouted. Her heart fluttered, just a little. "It's the Hansel and Gretel.[34] His new one. He toots it when he's tired of playing hide-and-seek. He's leaving a trail!"

Sal's mouth quirked. "A trail of toots?"

Mona nodded. "So we can find him."

"Th-the ocean is a big place to look," Wendell said.

Thea shrugged. "Our love's bigger than any ocean, though."

---

34 #224: The Hansel and Gretel: A trail of toots most often used in games of hide-and-seek with Toot's siblings, to help them find him quickly. Smells like marinara sauce and mildew.

Mona rolled her eyes. (But secretly she agreed.) "We have a trail of toots. We have a map. We have a water witch. Let's go!"

"Aren't you all forgetting something?" Sal said. "We have to build a boat. That could take weeks . . ."

"Alex!" Mona shouted his name. But when she looked at him, the sadness in his eyes gave her the answer they needed.

"That little boat's not built to withstand big tides. I'm sorry."

Sundae squeezed his hand.

The wind whipped Mona's hair again. Just ahead of her, the statue of Olivia the Great and Terrible held her lantern high. Beyond Olivia, the Lost Cove Library sat docked in the harbor.

"We're not going to build a boat," said Mona with a grin. "We're going to . . . borrow one."

"That's not a good idea," Sal said. "We don't know how to sail a giant ship. Also, we don't really know how to read Grandpa's map. It's a bunch of dots. We don't know how to navigate. Even you aren't that good with directions."

At this moment, a funny shadow eclipsed the Problim children. It stretched long, and appeared to be that of an astronaut with wings. Mona squinted into the smiling face of Violet O'Pinion. Their cousin. They were family now. Did Violet know too? Had she figured it out already?

Biscuit bounced up beside her owner, wearing a tiny life jacket, bopping her tiny tail.

"I'm great with maps," Violet said, sun shining through the worlds on her wings. "I'll come with you."

Mona smirked. "Okay, then. Problms, pile up."

Acknowledgments

I'm especially grateful to Suzie Townsend (my incredible agent) and Maria Barbo (my editor extraordinaire) for their encouragement, expert advice, and for helping the Problim children come alive in Lost Cove. I'm also grateful to Cassandra Baim and the creative wizards at New Leaf Literary & Media. A volley of thank you toots are owed to Katherine Tegen, Stephanie Guerdan, and the wonderful team at HarperCollins/Katherine Tegen Books. I can't believe I get to work with so many people who love—and treasure—the power of a story.

I'm also grateful to the myriad of librarians, teachers, booksellers, bloggers and book lovers who've helped my stories find homes in readers' hearts. On that note, I wish I could give endless boxes of donuts and dancing spiders to Star Lowe, the owner of my hometown indie bookstore, Star Line Books, for championing the Problims (and their author) at every turn.

Endless thanks to my family, for loving me through every page of the stories I write, as well as the story I'm living. My husband, Justin (whom I love more than a charm of hummingbirds), and my dogs, Biscuit and Samson, who don't seem remotely troubled about how often I discuss fictional people. For that, and for the billion other wonderful ways they light up my life, I love them more than words. I'm grateful to my parents—first, for bringing me Starbucks, second, for their eagerness to read new drafts, and third, for proudly calling me an author long before any of my stories were published. I am grateful to God for family, friends, and the wild wonder of imagination.

And I am deeply grateful to—and for—young readers. It's an absolute honor to write stories for you. Like the Problims, I hope you stay kind and curious, brave and courageous.

The Problim Children series
by Natalie Lloyd

> "*The Problim Children* is bursting at the seams with magic, heart, and humor. A sheer, riotous delight."
> —Claire Legrand, author of *Some Kind of Happiness*

NORTHERN PLAINS
PUBLIC LIBRARY
Ault, Colorado

 KATHERINE TEGEN BOOKS
An Imprint of HarperCollins Publishers

www.harpercollinschildrens.com